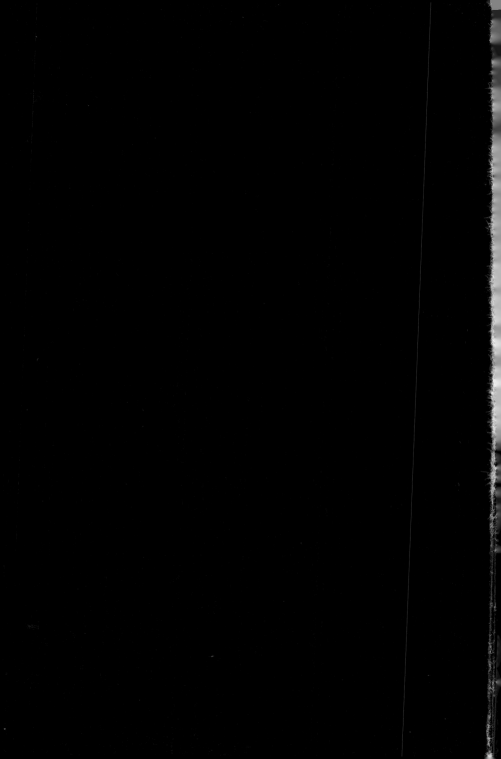

BEFORE
WE GO
EXTINCT

Karen Rivers

BEFORE WE GO EXTINCT

Farrar Straus Giroux
New York

For Peter Benchley, who changed my life with his book

Farrar Straus Giroux Books for Young Readers
175 Fifth Avenue, New York 10010

Text copyright © 2016 by Karen Rivers
All rights reserved
Printed in the United States of America
Designed by Andrew Arnold
First edition, 2016
1 3 5 7 9 10 8 6 4 2

fiercereads.com

Library of Congress Control Number: 2015034448

ISBN 978-0-374-30240-5

Our books may be purchased in bulk for promotional, educational, or
business use. Please contact your local bookseller or the Macmillan Corporate
and Premium Sales Department at (800) 221-7945 ext. 5442 or by e-mail
at MacmillanSpecialMarkets@macmillan.com.

BEFORE WE GO EXTINCT

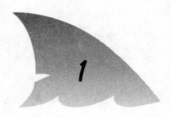

1

MY FOOT IS STUCK IN THE TOILET BOWL IN THE CLOSET-
sized bathroom in the two-bedroom walk-up I live in with my mom
on the corner above Alf's Bodega.

I fell in hard, footfirst. I was trying to see the roof of the For
Reel Fish Market, checking for shark fins drying out there in the
hotter-than-it-should-be June sun.

It's not that I don't like the owner, Mrs. Stein, I do. I just
thought maybe she was cashing in so she could move to Florida.
There's more money in shark fins, pound for pound, than anything
else in the sea. Somewhere along the line I stopped trusting everyone, even the lady who gives me free shrimp when I walk by, calls
me "boychick," and cried when I broke my arm trying to take off
from the fire hydrant out front when I was five.

Spoiler: people can't fly.

Mrs. S. has an old yellowed photo of Key West taped to the
peeling wall over the cash register. She talks about how she'd do
anything she could to get there, to have that life, to smell those

flowers and the sunscreen and sea salt. In the Keys, it's all sand and rusty bikes and tropical drinks and music. She won't take her troubles with her. There will be no Mr. S. scratching his eczema-encrusted arms and grunting and no customers shouting about the price of crab these days. It will be so perfect, empty, free, and blue that she maybe wouldn't feel guilty about her part in destroying the ocean's balance and depleting the atmosphere of oxygen, killing us all.

The truth is, that's what's happening and no one cares. The sharks will be all fished out sooner than you think, the balance of the food chain will be tipped. You think it doesn't matter, but it does. Most of our oxygen comes from plankton in the sea. If there isn't enough oxygen, our lungs will fill up with carbon dioxide. The end. The failure of the species.

The failure of us.

Not tomorrow, not next week, but soon enough that we *should* be panicking. We should be doing everything we can to stop it. But we aren't. We're going to let it happen. We'll just sit here and slowly die, pacified by our own dumb existences that don't even matter. Not really. Not to the whole big world.

As it happens, there aren't any shark fins on the Steins' roof, and now my foot is wedged into the bowl at an angle that looks like a joke picture someone should post on social media. But it sure doesn't feel like a joke, and I don't post stuff like that and LOL. Not anymore. *#becausenothingisfunnynow*

If there had been even one triangular hunk of flesh up there, I could have been a hero, shutting down another illegal finning operation, just like the guy who made that movie *Sharkwater*. That movie changed my life. The movie that turned me into Sharkboy, which turned into Sharky. The movie that I happened to see before my first day at the Richer-Than-You Academy for Famous People's Kids and One Charity Case—guess which one I am?—so that when they put me on the spot and told me that I had to introduce my-self to the school by doing an impromptu speech about something I cared about, the sharks were right there, still sinking, bleeding, finless, in my mind and it was all I could think to talk about. I didn't think I'd *cry*. People don't forget stuff like that, as it turns out: the new guy, six feet tall, sweating into his hair, nervous, then bursting into real, actual tears at the podium on their fancy stage.

Because we're all going to die!

Yeah? Sissy.

But if you think about it, what better thing is there to cry about? People? You want to cry about *people* dying? Why?

It happens.

People die. No one is immortal. We're just a bunch of organs stuffed into a skin sack, waiting for something to fail.

Waiting to fall.

After that, the sharks and I were forever linked. I was Shark-boy to most people; Great White to The King, which was kind of two types of jokes: one about my race, and one about the shark of the same name. There were ruder things to be called. They could have gone with Crybaby, or worse. And me, well, I *like* being lumped in with the sharks. Sharks have always been my favorite things. Think about it. They are amazing in a hundred different ways. A thousand.

Besides, the ocean is my kind of place, full of silence and

mysteries and species people haven't even discovered yet. Things that have never been seen, never been co-opted by humans, never been destroyed by greed. We always kill the stuff that matters. Who needs outer space when we have so much we don't understand yet right here, our own secret universe that we mostly ignore, take for granted, and throw plastic garbage into, destroying everything?

Not me. I don't take anything for granted.

I flip my cell phone around and around in my hand, slapping it against my palm over and over. My sweaty fingers leave marks on the screen. I can feel my pulse in my foot, thrumming like the music I can sometimes feel coming up through the floor from 3B. Not today though. Today, it's quiet.

I'd call someone to help me out here, but I stopped talking a while back and I can't think when or why I'll ever start again. *My foot is stuck in the toilet* doesn't seem like reason enough to break this impenetrable barrier that I've made by being silent for so long that it's gelled like that and no one can reach all the way through. It's a lot like being underwater and there's a reason why fish don't make sounds.

Besides, there's always texting.

Help, I type with my greasy finger. *I've fallen and I can't get up.* I take a picture of my foot down there, a million miles away, white sock in blue water. *#footinthebowl #awkward #helpme* Then I run it through a filter that makes it look like Mrs. Stein's Florida snapshot: white border, water turned aquamarine. She doesn't just want to go to Florida, she wants to go to Florida in 1960, through a time travel machine that erases all the crappy big box stores that make every city in America virtually the same as every other one. Not that I'd ever tell her that. What does it hurt that she believes that *that* Florida still exists? She'll never get there. Most people spend their whole lives dreaming of a future that never comes.

There's nothing wrong with dreaming. I'd like to do a little time traveling myself. I'd like to go back exactly twenty-four days, give or take an hour or two. I'd like to do something completely different on that day. I'd like to change everything.

I tap Send. The phone makes that sound that makes me think of carrier pigeons, swooping between buildings with my message strapped to their leg. They'll have a long way to fly to get it to The King, who is buried in a graveyard in Connecticut, where his dad and wife Number Seven have a summer place that they go to on hot long weekends to drink their pompous sparkling drinks, clattering with ice cubes. It's what counts as hobbies to those people: congratulating themselves for being rich, smugly offering each other handshakes and air kisses like they are blessings from the pope, and drinking, always sipping something from a goblet held in their manicured hands.

I think they buried The King's phone with him. I bet it's buzzing right now, down there in the marble box where he is lying.

#LOL, I type, even though nothing is funny.

Swoop, swoop.

I finally yank my stupid foot out of the bowl—which is harder than you'd think it would be, a crunching and popping comes from the joint and I feel it in my stomach—and push the handle, wishing I could flush my whole self. I'd disappear and be gone for good, spat out into the sea where I'd swim away from shore instead of toward it, swim and swim and swim until finally a fin would surface beside me, then another, and there I'd be, surrounded. And for some reason, they would be saying, *Thanks, Sharkboy, thanks.* And I'd be like, *Think nothing of it, friends.* (This is a fantasy, so obviously being able to speak to sharks is totally a given.) And that would be that, me floating there on my back, ears filled up with water, muffling everything. Me, in the gray waves, staring up at the sky, and the sharks swimming around and around and around, slipping through the water like something too graceful to exist on land, something too beautiful. All of us out there together, away from this, so far away that somehow we'd be saved.

2

LET'S GET THIS PART STRAIGHT:

No matter what you might have heard or read on the Internet, falling was not in The King's plan when he fell from the steel beam jutting out of the forty-second floor of his dad's newest building, which was under construction on Eleventh and Fifty-Third, three Tuesdays ago at 4:27 in the afternoon. What the media hacks didn't mention was we did that all the time. Not the falling, you understand. Obviously. But it was where we hung out. The husks of incomplete skyscrapers were our playground. We skateboarded on the huge, empty floors. We balanced on the steel beams. We ran up the walls, leaving dusty footprints higher than you'd think would be possible, backflipping off. We taught ourselves parkour because the buildings were there and we had the keys and why not? It felt just dangerous enough. Sometimes we didn't make it, we'd lie in the dust bleeding but high from it all the same. We flew from one side of the building to another, careering off piles of tiles, toolboxes, scrap metal, or Sheetrock. Then, when we got tired of that, we'd get daring. Like superheroes who never actually did anything heroic, we'd stand above the city, above everyone. We'd look down, fighting the part of our brain that wanted us to get away from the edge, to stay away from all the edges. We clawed it back, that's what it felt like, like you were actually tearing your sanity away to force yourself to stand there, looking down. There was adrenaline in our knees and our guts but doing it felt like *winning*. Nothing would happen but also everything could. Anything.

It felt like absolute power, if you want to know the truth. Being able to get past that part of you that says *stop*. Pushing through and past. It felt like infinity would feel if it could be a feeling. It was everything.

The King would stand out there and yell down to the street, "YOU WALK IN OUR SHADOWS, PEASANTS." He wasn't being a jerk. Not really. He was just being a voice, a huge voice that was like weather, like anything immutable and imperfect and enormous. He was this tiny little guy, but his voice was the voice of a giant. Anyway, no one could hear him, not from that far away. Afterward, we'd lie back on the concrete floors, howling like wolves, dust in our mouths, in our lungs, the bruises pressed into our skin like victory scars. After a while, it became a normal thing.

Our normal.

It might be a different normal from most people's but that doesn't make it any less true.

After a while, it was *normal* the way sometimes it felt like you were falling, even when you weren't, the street pulsing up toward you and then away, the yellow cabs like rows of bright plastic ants, swirling in the sweet chaos of your vertigo.

It was *normal* to force yourself to sit down, legs dangling, your shoes looking like seagulls flying miles above the ground.

That's how I know what happened that day was an accident.

Which means that Daff is a liar.

It's been twenty-one days since I spoke to Daffodil Blue of "He died because of *love!*" *Gawker* fame. She was an instant Internet darling, with her red lips puffed up like shiny new Volkswagen Beetles, glistening on the screen, all those fake tears spilling from her overly made-up eyes. It helps that her dad is so famous: Big Doc, a rap producer ("crap producer," as she'd say). She was born to this, born famous, like The King, just waiting for her chance to appear on your screens, biting her lip, looking up through her lashes, daring you to comment on her ridiculously puffy head of hair.

And instantly, she became one of *them*, one of the people we hated, layers of fake nothingness concealing an empty bubble. She became someone who wasn't Daff. She became *Daffodil Blue*: the quirky beautiful rich kid that the weird ugly rich kid had killed himself over.

For love, don't you know?

But that's a *lie*.

It was an *accident*.

I know it was.

I was there.

"Je suis désolé," was the last thing that I said to her, right before I sidestepped away from her fake take-pictures-of-me hug and walked out the church door where the sun outside was burning the pigeons' feet on the sidewalk and people wilted downward to subways that might take them away from the heat. I walked only a few yards

11

before my knees started to liquefy and I knelt right there on those famous stone steps and fought the urge to press my face into the filthy pavement, to push through it to the other side.

There were media vans parked up and down the road, reporters hanging around with microphones and cameras so maybe they could get a sound bite from The King's dad afterward, maybe a glimpse of a real tear on the great man's famous, chiseled African face or the equally famous faces of his plastic, soulless friends. And yeah, they might get a tear from this actress or that model, but it's not like *he'd* cry. As if.

To cry, he'd have to be human.

A few of them stared at me, too hot to bother raising their lenses for the most part, but a couple of cameras caught me. You probably saw that shot, too. I guess some jackass won an award for that image of me bent over on my knees on the steps of the church, looking at the gray hard stone that my black rubber-soled school shoes were melting on.

My knees burned.

What I was thinking then, at that exact moment, were the words *pink mist*.

Pink mist.

Pink. Mist.

See, I did this paper on 9/11 last year for my Social History class. I had to read all the news stories, eyewitness accounts, details. The *details* are what get to you when you start to look closely at things like that. One guy said that when people jumped out of the Twin Towers, they fell so hard onto the pavement that a pink mist was coming up off the ground.

Pink mist.

I threw up all over the church stairs, my puke running in rivulets between the stones. It surprised me as much as any of the gawking journalists. I haven't vomited since I was a little kid. It hurt, acid in my nose, the whole bit. Someone's cigarette butt moved along in my river of steaming puke, which made little tributaries around a piece of chewed gum. A candy wrapper. Cigarette butts ground into two-dimensional images of themselves. When I finally got up and walked past the reporters, no one looked me in the eye. My kind of mourning wasn't camera-ready, I guess.

I wasn't famous.

I was nobody.

The King has now been gone for twenty-four days. He was more than just the strange-looking kid of an obnoxiously rich real estate tycoon. He was The King. He was complicated, funny, smart, crazy, kind, brilliant, and sometimes a total jerk. He was my best friend. And no one knew him like I did.

But now he's nothing.

He's dead. A body in a box underground.

Well, what's left of a body.

Pink mist.

Dead is a word like a smooth marble you've put in your mouth to see what it was like and then inhaled by mistake leaving your windpipe suddenly and perfectly blocked. I wonder if the dead try to breathe right after they die, not knowing yet that they can't, that they won't. Not ever again. I wonder what that must feel like, knowing that the air isn't coming in to fill you up, not this time.

I wonder when The King stopped breathing.

If he thought, What happened?

When he fell, there was a *whoomp* as the wind filled his white school shirt. It billowed so big, a cleanly laundered sheet against the clouds, like a parachute in cartoons. For a split second, I thought he might be lifted back up into the sky.

For a split second, he looked beautiful.

But that thin white shirt didn't even slow him down. He was gone so fast, he couldn't have really thought anything. He probably didn't even hear me screaming. He probably couldn't even see me standing there, helpless, doing nothing.

He didn't know there wasn't anything I could do to save him.

3

THE PHONE IN MY HAND VIBRATES.

Daff: *R U there?*

I squeeze my eyes shut like you do when you're a kid and you don't want anyone to see you. I half wish I had a blanket fort to crawl into, to hide away in for good. Maybe with a glass of milk and some cookies and some Lego guys and a video game and a life that is not this life.

Not *my* life.

Non, I type. *Je ne suis pas ici maintenant.*

French seems to be the only way I can type back to her without saying anything, the only way I can answer without being myself.

I put the phone in the sink and turn on the tap, hard, water splashing off it and onto the mirror, onto me. But it's one of those phones that are waterproof, which, as it happens, The King gave me for my birthday. He said my old flip phone was embarrassing to everyone. "Seriously," he said. "No one needs to see that." Like my flip phone was actually insulting people's eyes. I'd taken it, but the gift stung. Did my phone matter? What else mattered? That I didn't have anything and that he was as rich as Trump? How soon was it going to be that money mattered more than all the other stuff we had, all the other stuff we did? Our dusty footprints that were twin shadows up on the brick walls, the jokes that no one else got, the way we moved through the school like it was ours, and so, we owned it. We got each other. That was a pretty big thing. Not everyone gets you in life. Not everyone understands. But we were tight and we were untouchable: me, Daff, and The King. Undisputed royalty of the School of the Sons and Daughters of Rich Pricks (and me).

I wonder who is going to pay the monthly phone bill now that he's gone, how long it will take his dad's accountant to realize that The King couldn't possibly be using it anymore. The water sluices off the screen, leaving the greasy path of my fingerprints behind.

The gulls on the Steins' roof laugh cruelly. Someone on the street yells in hard-edged language and there's the sound of something heavy and metallic falling, a silence, then a barking laugh. Then a honk and a squeal of tires. The roar of a bus going by. More laughter. (How dare you *laugh*, I think. How dare you. The King is dead. Are you stupid? Don't you *know*?) That's how I feel about all of it, like the whole world should stop laughing, even the seagulls. Don't they get it? We are all on our way out.

Music with too much bass reverberates from the window across the gap. I read once somewhere that so much bass eventually does something to the muscles in your colon and people who listen that way will end up in adult diapers sooner or later. I make a mental note to stick some coupons for Depends on the guy's front door. Jerk. He deserves it.

I turn the water off and pick up my phone and wipe it on my pant leg. I like the heft of it in my hand. That stupid phone makes me feel connected to everything and everyone, even to the people it can't connect me to anymore.

It makes me feel safe.

There are footsteps in the hall, then Mom knocks. I shove the phone into my pocket, quick, like she can see through walls and doors, like she knows I'm texting a dead guy like someone who is too stupid to understand that dead is dead is a marble choking you to death.

I gag and spit in the sink. *Pink mist.*

"I need to talk to you about something important, JC," she says. "I wish you'd come out of there. I have to go to work in an hour. One hour, do you hear me? One. I can't miss this train. And I want to . . . I have to . . . Well, just come out, would you?"

Her voice wobbles a bit, which bugs me. It makes me mad. I'm still *me*. Why can't she see that? I'm so angry with her for treating me like I'm broken, even if I am.

Ahem, ahem, Mom coughs. *Ribbit ribbit.*

"Sharky?" Mom leans on the door and I can tell the full weight of her is there, pressing. The door is wood. Brown. Wood makes me think of coffins. The idea of coffins makes me feel like I am breathing through a straw with holes, nothing is filling up my lungs. I inhale and inhale and inhale until I'm dizzy, dizzier, the dizziest. The King's coffin isn't even wood, it's marble. There are stones inlaid across the top that look like actual jewels. I don't know what they are. Diamonds? Crystals? His coffin is worth more than everything I've ever owned in my life.

"Sweetheart?"

I shove the window open farther and gulp in the garbagey, fishy, hot-pavement scent of the alley. My lungs drown in the humid stench, that damp stink that seems to have stuck around long after they cleaned up Hurricane Sandy, like everything went moldy and now can never really be cleaned.

My mom sighs so loud I can practically feel it. "JC . . . ," she starts again. She rattles the knob. "What are you doing in there? Do I need to *do* something?" She delivers a solid kick to the door, which rattles but doesn't break. "Ouch," she says. "Shit. I mean, sugar."

I take my phone out of my pocket and type, *Am OK. Sorry,* and send it to her. The *swoop swoop* of those invisible birds carries it right through the door into her pocket and I hear her phone buzz and then I can hear her reading it. I know you shouldn't be able to hear someone read, but somehow, now, I can. Sharks can read the electrical impulses in the water; I can read the electrical impulses in the air.

Everything vibrates.

The last thing I said to The King was, "Hey, Chief Not Scared of Heights, you're going to fall." I was sort of laughing, sort of not. I took a picture. *#dontlookdown* He was too far out for it to be funny, maybe five or six feet from safety. That's not much when you're two feet off the ground, but when you are on the forty-second floor, trust me: it's a lot. He bounced a little on the balls of his feet, like he was going to start jogging. Then he wobbled, sat down. "HEY!" I yelled. "Seriously."

He was looking at his phone. Typing.

"Don't text and drive!" I said, which was a joke because of this campaign at school about texting and driving that we all made fun of because we were kids in New York: none of us could *drive*.

Then my phone buzzed. I pulled it out of my pocket while I was yelling, "Come *on*. You're going to get blown off, dude."

I angled my phone to cut the glare on the screen and read it. It said *srry*. It was from The King. "What?" I said. "Dude. WHAT?"

The distance between me and The King stretched like melting plastic and then there was that forever second, my WHAT? hanging in the air between us, becoming as thin as a thread, breaking in the sky, long strings of it dangling down toward the ground like a jungle of plastic vines.

The King didn't hear me because of the wind and because he was already tipping backward, scuba diver–style. His face like the weather, all jumbled up: storm clouds, rain, lightning, and the sun.

I saw him raise his eyebrows and

It was really gusty by then, the wind was

Anyway he was already

Some things are too hard to

Screw this. I mean, seriously.

"Please," Mom says, from the other side of the door. "Please, Sharky."

OK ok ok, I type. I hesitate. I stare myself down in the mirror. Suck it up, Buttercup, I think. My cold dead eyes glare back at my cold dead eyes. My lips curl in a sneer. My face has forgotten how to arrange itself properly. I allow it to fall back into flat nothingness, expression free. When did I get so skinny? I can see the bones in my face, the skeleton of me pushing to get through.

I touch Send.

I peel my now-blue sock off and slop it, dripping blueness all over the clean tile, into the garbage can. Underneath, the skin of my foot is blue, too, and puckered. My ankle is starting to swell.

The phone vibrates.

Daff: *I need 2 talk 2 you.*

I type: *Je suis indisponible.*

I hear Mom move away from the door, her footsteps slapping the floor toward the kitchen. When I put weight on my ankle, it hurts like something separate from me, with a life of its own. I take a picture of it. *#bluefootedbooby* It's almost a funny thing to type right now. LOL LOL LOL.

My phone buzzes again. *Need 2 talk 2 you srsly <3 Daff. I have something from him. U have to c it. Its 4u.*

I almost send her the blue-foot pic. But then I don't. I hit Delete. I reply to her with my standard, *Non merci.* No thank you. No mercy. Whichever you prefer, m'lady. I love her so hard it hurts, like all my organs are curling over inside me. But I can't. Not now. Not ever.

I put my hand on the door and open it, dizzy, dizzy, dizzy. At any moment, I might just faint dead away, like one of those too-skinny girls in my class, folding up against the hall wall like a piece of beautiful paper. The light grays and thins. I pinch the skin of my wrist hard. The feeling passes.

It always passes.

I'm okay.

I'm fine.

I go into the kitchen and sit down.

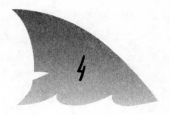

4

"HE PROBABLY FAINTED IN THE AIR," THE FAT COP HAD said. "I learned that back on September 11, you know, 2001. I was there, like . . . I was *there*. All those people, jumping, remember? Falling. Well, you're too young to remember. But all those *people*. It was unbelievable. Holding hands. That one woman holding down her skirt. Anyway, they said they all fainted, passed right out, didn't know what it was like to . . . Oh, I shouldn't be saying this, I guess. Shit. I'm sorry. Kid, I'm sorry."

He looked surprised, like I had made him say those things, like my friend *dying* had forced these words out of him against his will. I scowled. I wanted him to stop but I couldn't find the words. I couldn't find any words. Words were a school of fish flashing in the sun and then vanishing all at once, a hundred thousand bodies departing in one smooth motion.

He leaned so close to me I could smell that he ate a meatball sub for lunch, washed it down with a coffee and a piece of too-weak gum. He had a gold filling in the side of his front tooth with a hunk of dark food stuck beside it. I wanted to punch him hard, so hard his nose would burst, a cartoon balloon.

"It's something like two hundred miles an hour when you fall like that," the skinny cop interrupted, his face all creased up like rotten fruit. He sounded excited. "What McRory there means is that he didn't feel anything, ya know."

A word burned on the end of my tongue. I opened my mouth. Nothing happened. I tried again. "Screw you," I croaked, real quiet. And then, just like that my voice was drained out of me, like blood pooling on the ground. I could feel it go, heavy like syrup. I expected to look down and see under my chair a puddle of words I'd never say.

The fat cop squinted at me. Then, his eyes on my eyes, he reached over and touched my face. His fingertip was soft and terrible. I froze, every part of me clenched up, wanting to fight or to flee. My throat snapped tight shut in a way that made me think of gulls, swallowing. I started to gag. He pulled his hand back, looked at it like it wasn't anything to do with him, operating without permission. He shook his head again, hard. Like an Etch A Sketch he was trying to erase.

That one woman holding down her skirt. Holding hands. Fainted in the air.

Mom took me home from the station in a cab that cost forty-two dollars.

The forty-twos were everywhere. I couldn't get away from them.

I Googled the thing about fainting first thing when I got into my room and I found out that it's just an urban legend. You don't pass out when you fall from high up. People want to think that because it makes the trip down to the ground seem more palatable to the witnesses. And cops are liars, like everyone else.

I guess The King was awake right until he wasn't.

File that under: Things I Don't Want to Know.

It's right there in my brain, next to my other ever-growing file: Things I Can't Stop Seeing.

His shirt billowing against the backdrop of the sky.

The crowd on the sidewalk when I finally got there.

Pink mist.

My own face in the mirror, staring back at me.

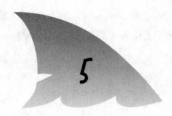

5

MOM'S EYES ARE TIRED BUT THAT DOESN'T MEAN THEY
aren't perfectly lined and shadowed, each eyelid like a tiny art
canvas, a black mole that looks like cancer perfectly drawn on her
powdered, death-white cheek. The table is bright yellow. She painted
it last year when she wasn't tired yet, when she was still reinventing
the apartment as often as she reinvented herself.

I am why she is so tired.

The bright yellow paint is bubbling. I stick my fingernail under
the edge and start to peel it, which I know drives her crazy, but that
yellow is offensively cheerful. Underneath the yellow is a flat gray-
brown that seems a lot more like real life. She turns off the music
and the silence is sudden, like jumping into the sea and having your
ears fill up.

Last summer, I took diving classes at the Y. We learned to
breathe through regulators. We swam around the swimming pool,
looking at each other's legs, picking up coins from the faded blue
tiles. On the one day when we actually dove in Long Island Sound,

a storm came up and we had to come in. We only got fifteen minutes down there. It was the worst, best fifteen minutes of my life. The seaweed was covered with slime that looked like sewage. The one fish I saw was dead, trapped in a roll of wire someone had dumped off the side of their boat. The water was the kind of filthy that made me think I'd see corpses: suited men with ties flapping, feet encased in concrete.

Or bull sharks, hungry for a meal.

Saltwater crocs, rising from the murk.

Everything was gray-brown. Like life. Like the table. Like everything we are pretending not to be.

It scared me: the way the ocean was struggling to be alive but failing, the way a rusty oil can lay under litter and old tires. I hated it mostly for not being what I expected, for not looking like a National Geographic special, or like footage from the *Shark Week* episodes that I watched over and over again.

I wasn't expecting coral reefs, I'm not a total idiot. But I was expecting something else.

Something beautiful.

Something *other*.

At least something more colorful.

I couldn't explain it after, to Mom, so I said it was great. The best. Everything I wanted. Luckily, scuba diving is something I can't really afford to do and we live in *Brooklyn*. It's not exactly the Great Barrier Reef.

One day, when I have enough saved up, I'll fly somewhere where the diving is amazing. I'll go to Australia. I'll sign up for a dive. I'll step into that water and swim as far away from the reef as I can.

I'll look down into the deep and see the answer to some question that I haven't thought up yet. I'll see the heft of the shadows gliding through the water below me and I'll know exactly what they are. And what they are doing.

I'll understand them.

And they'll understand me.

That's when it will make sense.

Mom takes a deep breath and lets it out slowly, like someone in pain. In, out. In, out. A third time. Giving birth to a sentence. I kind of know how she feels, but it's also annoying. Pant, pant, pant.

Then finally she blurts, "I know the timing is rotten but the show is filming on location for the summer to try to boost ratings by, you know, spicing it up with 'world travel' . . . I—I'm going. I just, well, I have to tell you. I'm going to go. I have to go. It's a thing I have to do." It comes out as one long word that sounds like a different language. I nod. *Yes, Mom. I understand.* She exhales so long that I can smell the toothpaste on her breath, laced with green tea and something stale.

Mom does makeup for a reality TV show about love that has nothing to do with reality. Or love. She paints contour marks on the main guy's abs. I forget his name this season, but it doesn't much matter. They are all the same, these guys. Gleefully smacking their lips at the sight of the women they get to pick from. This one guy licked his lips so often that he chapped the skin all the way up to his nose. Mom said it was gross to cover it up and he kept licking off the makeup. *Literally* licking his lips. Mankind is just so obvious, you know?

She makes shadows on the hopeful girls' cleavage. Like, what are they hoping for? A chance to be with this jerk? I don't get it, but it's basically the most popular show in the world, so what do I know? She hides their faces with the same thick mask of makeup. No one is real.

The saddest part is that those girls? They remind me of the new Daff. Painted on. Fake. Pretending.

It's the worst. I don't even watch it anymore. I used to watch it with Daff and we'd laugh our butts off about how gross it was, and how pathetic those people were. Now she's practically one of them. It's just a matter of time. Probably she'll be on it one day, fake crying about true love to the camera.

Mom pauses. Clears her throat, *ribbit ribbit*.

"I have to tell you that you are going to go stay with your dad, which will probably be good for you actually, to get away from here after, you know, everything that's happened and besides it might be . . . an experience. Different, at least, from anything you ever . . . you can just take some time . . . and . . . well. You know. And . . . and you and your dad need to reconnect and the show says I can't bring you with me and I'm sorry, Sharky, but your dad is your dad no matter what and he loves you and maybe this trip is going to be the best thing to happen to you after all."

It's like she thinks that if she stops to take any more breaths, I'll be able to stop her from saying what she's saying. I'll somehow be able to change her mind.

I'm super aware of my own breathing now. In, out. In, out. In, out. Pant, pant, pant. It just keeps going, a person's inhalations and exhalations, while all around them their life might be completely changing. In and out, like you can't stop yourself. Something metallic is in my mouth that tastes like blood or hate. I work up some saliva and swallow it down. I go over to the sink and spit. I fill a glass with water. The pipes belch.

"I've sublet the apartment to that girl Blaire who answers the phones at the studio," she adds. "She has cats. She's too young to have that many cats. But I know her, so I thought it would be better than—well. I hope they don't scratch all the furniture but I guess it doesn't . . . we can just lock your room and I'll pile some other stuff in there and . . . I rented it, anyway, as a one bed. I couldn't tell you, I didn't know how to tell you, I know you're upset, you should be upset, I am upset. This has all been very upsetting . . ." Her voice trails off. Her eyes are on the wall behind me, which is bare except for the one painting she did when she decided to go to art school when I was five, a painting of a kid in bright red boots standing ankle deep in the waves at the beach, staring out to sea. The sea has highlights of purple and green and red, it's hardly blue at all. Mom can never see things as they are. The kid is me, I guess, but I never had red boots.

"It's just that," she says, "I'm not sure how to do this, JC. I'm not sure how to be a parent to you right now. I don't know what you need or how to do it. I've run out of—I just don't . . . I don't know, Sharky. I love you, but I don't know how to do this. You need someone. Something. Someone else."

I am shaking my head slowly side to side. No way. My heart is thumping out something that I can't explain, which is Daff, Daff, Daff, Daff.

No.

"Sharky," she says. "Sharkboy. JC, sweetie. Come on. Don't

make it harder. I'm only—it's that I can't lose this job, and you know, I think . . ."

And suddenly, instantly, I am drowning. I am de-finned and sinking all the way to the bottom. I see stars. I am going to pass out and I am going to . . . and then suddenly my throat opens. I gulp in air, thirsty. She stares at me. "You okay?" she says. "It's just—I'm sorry. I'm late. I have to—well, I have to go. I can't get fired. Not now. Sh—I mean, sugar. I'm so late. *Sharky, I cannot be late.*"

Her temper starts bubbling up. Mom has some issues with anger.

"I HAVE TO GO," she shouts, as though I'm the one who has been keeping her here.

I shrug and listen to my pulse pick up speed and start galloping. When I was a kid and this happened, I used to faint. Mom would get mad about spilled milk or how I took too long to put on my shoes and I'd fade out to the tune of the horse hooves of my heart, cantering. I went to therapy.

Now I just listen to her and pretend her voice is waves, pouring over me. I'm a rock. I'm a reef. I'm the land.

I acknowledge that her anger isn't anything to do with me.

I keep breathing.

Stay in the moment.

"ARGH," she yells. "I'M SORRY, OKAY? I don't know why I'm so *mad!*"

I nod. I know she doesn't.

"Anyway," she says. "He's your *father*, okay? You can live with him for a couple of months. He's *your* dad."

But I hate him, is what I'd say if I talked.

No, I can't.

No way.

Not him.

No.

Please.

What about Daff?

I don't say anything. I flip my phone in my hand over and over and over. The sun shines on the screen and makes it a mirror. I stumble to the table and sit.

Mom pushes her chair back, gets up.

She walks away.

She says, "I'm sorry, sweetie. You know I love you. I hope I don't miss the bus because then I'll miss the stupid train again—I . . ."

I hear her pick up her keys, but I don't turn around.

I hear her fast-walking down the hall.

I flip my phone.

And just like that, it buzzes.

Daff. *If u wrnt there, u wldn't ansr, jrkfce.*

Daff has a vowel problem. Vowels have a Daff problem.

Non, I type. *Au revoir. Je ne regrette rien. Je regrette tout.*

I can't even explain to myself why I can't talk to her. There's nothing I want more than to talk to her. I love her. I hate her. I can't. I just can't.

The sun comes out and filters through the window, making a patch of shadows on the table that takes the glare off all that yellow. There is a bowl of apples in the middle of the table; they are Mom-level clean, probably bleached. I watch my hand reach out for one and I take it and bite into it and the flesh of it crisps against my teeth. It tastes like school lunches in third grade before anything bad happened. I put it back in the bowl, one bite missing. A bite I can't seem to swallow. I chew and chew. Tears are looming somewhere behind my eyes, threatening to struggle to the surface. A fly buzzes from over near the sink, settling on the drain board. I raise my hand, like I'm saying goodbye. Goodbye, fly. Goodbye, Mom. Goodbye, New York. Goodbye, The King. Goodbye, Daff. Goodbye goodbye goodbye.

"You have a few more weeks here," she'd said as she left the room. "You can get through them. I know it's hard. I know it's really *so* hard. But then it's summer and . . ." She'd spread her hands, expanding them as far as she could, like summer will be this thing that is big, big enough to make me forget.

The King died in the spring.

I look up at the ceiling. I don't know what I'm looking for. Bubbles to follow to the surface?

Or maybe for the light.

6

Dear Daff,

This letter is not in French.

I'm not going to send it, so don't worry about what it says
or what I think or feel because what does it matter anyway?
You should think about the stuff you're good at thinking
about now, like how you look better with your hair frizzed
out than if you straighten it with that hot-iron thing. You
should think about your jeans, which ones make you look
the skinniest. (You aren't fat. I don't know why I said that.)

(I am trying to hurt you, because I'm so angry.)

(You look beautiful.)

(You look terrible.)

That's what you're thinking about, right? How to look
good on TV?

You do look good.

I hate you. (Which is why I sound mean.) I love you.
When I said that, I really meant it, not in the way you said

it back. Someone should write a book about the difference between I love you *and* love ya.

Anyway. You can't tell someone else how to feel, right? You can't make them feel what they don't. You don't get to decide. Yada yada. We've seen the shows. I'm basically the second-place girl who just can't freakin' believe that Mr. Overly Made-Up Abs isn't going to drop to his knees and propose and instead he's saying, "We had a connection right from the start and you're beautiful and I can't believe how lucky I am to know you but . . ." Everything in the world is contained in that but *and actually it's just a stupid TV show and none of them stay married and I wasn't going to* propose. *I just thought you should know because it was important and maybe it would have been different if The King hadn't died the next day.*

Maybe.

Or maybe that gave me something bigger to hurt about.

You looked beautiful in that photo on the Internet.

You used to not look quite as good. At least not, public consumption *good. But then again, you also used to think about things that matter. The world. The orphans in Nepal. The elephants being tortured. The way that people stopped connecting and started staring at their phones instead. The way AIDS is still a thing even though it gets less press. The women in the Congo. The sharks.*

You cared about everything.

Do you even remember?

Now, I guess, you're another famous face.

How did it happen so fast? That's what I want to know. It makes me feel kind of crazy, how quick you became someone else.

I guess I did, too.

But The King wins if it's a contest because he became dead.

That's the most profound transformation. You're only first runner-up.

I'm nothing.

I saw an interview with you on some stupid website. They called you an up-and-comer, but they didn't say in what. "The scene"? What does that even mean?

What scene?

It sounds like something you would hate.

Are you even old enough for "the scene"? What do your parents think of that?

And when did you start drinking in clubs? Was it like the day of the funeral? Did the invites start coming in?

I mean, seriously, what?

You know what I think about mostly?

I think about those finless sharks being thrown over the edges of the boats and the way they flick their tails in a sea of their own blood—that has to be exciting to their senses, all that blood, before they realize it's their own—the way the nerves in their bodies are sending a message to the place where their tail fins used to be, willing the nonexistent tail fins to move. The phantom tail fins. The way they try a few times before they realize it's not going to work. That nothing's going to work. Then they sink.

    They surrender to it.

    I wonder how that feels.

    I get the feeling I know how it feels.

    But you know what? I also think about the other stuff.

    I think about that party we went to at Parrish's place when his parents were on a cruise and he and his sister decorated the crap out of that apartment. If anyone else did that, we'd think, "Dude, seriously? Are you eight?" But somehow they made those fairy and wizard decorations seem purposeful and awesome, after all.

    I don't want to

    I mean, this is

    There are over three hundred different species of shark.

    I am trying to only think about sharks because it's easier, you know?

    It's easier than thinking about you. And about how you danced when you put the wings on at that party, the way that you were laughing. It was like a movie, a stupid romantic movie, when you spun around and around and the lights were flashing and for a second we were the only ones in the room and we weren't just slightly drunk teen-agers, we were every age we'd ever been: little kids, big kids, teenager, even our future adult selves, all spinning in that moment.

    Or maybe I was drunker than I thought.

I wanted to kiss you so bad, like I'd never wanted to kiss anyone before.

Then The King built that insane tightrope from the top of the stairs over the entrance hall and climbed onto it. Then he pasted on his look-at-me face. And then there was the way everyone stared like he knew they would, hooting and clapping.

The way, when he was done, you ran over to him and jumped on him, knocking him to the ground. That's when he grinned for real.

"Give the people what they want," he said to me from the floor, staring up, holding you tight around the waist like he'd never let you go. It was the way his hands were there on the bare part of your back above your jeans, the part that made me think of violins and sex.

I felt sick.

We had this deal that no one ever said out loud, but the deal was that we were friends, the three of us, and no one could cross the lines of friendship with you. Not me. Not him.

We had a deal.

Maybe you didn't know that. Or maybe you forgot.

Maybe he didn't know either.

So anyway, guess what?

I'm going to stay with my dad for a while.

Well, you know what he's like.

So really looking forward to that.

By which I mean, I'd rather do anything else. I'd say that I'd rather die, but that would be a lie and something that

I'm actually not going to say again because it's not funny anymore. Not ever. No matter who says it.

Anyway, no matter how much I think about them, those finned sharks can't be saved. Even if you were right there and caught them in your hands and held them up, they'd die anyway. They'd bleed out. You can't put a Band-Aid on a shark.

There's a lot of stuff you can't put a Band-Aid on.

I love you.

I hate you.

Whatever, right?

Smell ya later. Catch ya on the flip side. Love ya.

JC

I NEED TO SAY THAT SHE'S TOTALLY HILARIOUS.

And smart.

She is so smart.

She reads everything, just because. She read the encyclopedias up until the letter *M* and then she says it got repetitive and it felt like the earlier letters, the things she knew about, say, Alexandria, were leaking out to make room for Mars.

She took a night class at some old-person community center about Ancient Greece because she thought it looked "fun" but no one else signed up so it got canceled so she took knitting instead and made me a sweater with sleeves so long that I could put my legs in them and wear it like pants.

When she's tired, her left eye totally droops. When she sees that squint in pictures she posts them, tagged *#DirtyOldManWink*. She has a tattoo of a cartoon rabbit on her ankle that looks like a rat until you see the long ears. She can belt out a song like you wouldn't believe, her voice so gravelly and huge it'll make you think of big skies filled with stars or sex or the bottom of the sea.

Sex, mostly though.

I mean, come on. Seriously.

She's beautiful. She's so beautiful that if you look at her in the light of the biology lab, the sun streaming in and making everything look coated with dust, she'll look so stupidly beautiful, you'll think sappy things like, *She looks like an angel.* And you'll believe yourself.

If you aren't in love with her, there's something wrong with you.

But forget it, because she's saving herself for college. She says high school relationships are doomed to be remembered only when you're drunk. And when you think of them sober, you'll cringe and die a little inside, so she doesn't want to give herself something to regret.

Sometimes she spits when she's talking because she gets going so fast the words don't have a chance to leave the saliva behind and she has that gap between her front teeth. "The spit hole," she calls it. "Très très sexy." She once puked on Janet Jackson's lap at a celebrity wedding they both attended that ended in a pretty famous divorce less than a month later. (Janet said, "That's okay, sweetie," and patted her fluffy hair and then sent her parents a bill for three thousand dollars.)

She totally gets irony. She loves her parents as much as she hates their jobs and money. She knows the Japanese word for when the sun goes through the trees and the German word for being sick of everything in the world.

She makes these Buddhist sand mandala things for fun on the deck on the roof of her penthouse apartment building and waits for them to blow away in the wind because she says it's only when they are destroyed that they mean anything.

Who *says* stuff like that?

I thought she knew everything.

I thought she had the answers.

I thought she was someone she isn't.

As in, not the person she is pretending to be lately, the one who suddenly has a reason to be interviewed. "I've always wanted to be an actress," she says shyly.

Liar.

That's what I say. She never wanted to be an actress. She never wanted to be one of them.

Or maybe she was just lying to me.

I don't get it though. How can one person change so much, so fast?

Love is another one of those words that has a shape and a taste and a feel and way too much meaning and a bitter aftertaste, like grapefruit or some kind of rare Asian fruit with spines on it that you can only buy in the month of February and even then, only from that one weird little grocery store hidden in the shadows of a building on Twelfth. It's a word that sweats out of you, looking for a way to get away before anyone can really get hold of it, like a snake or mercury.

The thing with that prickly rare fruit is that once you've bitten it, you can't stop craving it. You think you'll go crazy for it, waiting for it to come back to you again.

I only kissed her once and it was an accident, that's what she said after. She's not totally wrong. I mean, sometimes when you stand too close to someone and their face is there, you have no real choice but to kiss it and anyway, you've had a beer and she smells good and you don't know that just letting your lips fall onto someone else's will turn into a body count.

How could you have known?

You should have known.

Of course he loved her, too.

The really stupid part is how much all of you laughed about that dumb show that your mom works on. How you were like, "This is so fake, man. This is so lame." How none of you really got how real it feels, even if it is all wrong. Even if it's hidden behind a bunch of crappy production values and thick makeup.

Right?

It's so stupidly human, that's the thing.

8

I COME OUT OF THE SCHOOL AND INTO A BLAST OF HOT sun an hour after everyone else, which sucks because now it's rush hour and the 6 train will be a nightmare of body odor and strangers' sweat dripping into your personal space. My commute takes two hours at this time of day and sometimes I like it because it gives me time to become the person I'm meant to be at the end of it. On hot days at rush hour, though, I'd rather light myself on fire than get onto one of those trains where even the windows are sweating back everyone's sweat, like a body odor sauna and the air-conditioning doesn't even begin to make a difference. If spring has been shockingly, unnaturally hot, now that it's officially summer, it's incendiary. It takes me a minute to adjust from the ice-cold office to this crazy heat, this oven of unforgivingly still air. It takes me another minute to think of where I can go. What I can do so that I don't leave here until late enough that the crowds will have cooled off, the train will be less of a horror show.

I don't know what to do.

The school is giving me grief counseling. It's mandatory. I think they're worried that The King's death will make me kill myself, like a grisly misguided Romeo-and-Juliet bromance. And while the Obnoxious School for the Overfunded *loves* to be on the news, they don't want it to be for some kind of lame suicide epidemic. If I don't do the counseling, they revoke my scholarship. They are serious about this. I mean, obviously for my own good, etc.

The counselor, "call me Ah-knee," is a person who has probably never experienced grief and who thinks I need to expel my negative energy by holding a crystal in my fist and humming one note over and over in a darkened room. It's so crazy that I want to laugh but I can't because The King is dead and it isn't funny because nothing is and at least the school has air-conditioning, which is more than I can say about our apartment. When I go home, I leave behind everything, all the best things like cool, metallic, machine-made air. I lose things like privilege and personal space. I become one of a million hot bodies destined for somewhere else, going back to where we belong, our little cheap boxes somewhere far away from this shiny, rich place.

I wonder how much "Ah-knee" charges. Where she lives. I bet she has an apartment overlooking the park. I bet the air conditioner blows so hard that her Persian cat's hair blows back in the cold air. I bet her doorman holds the door extra long for her, his eyes lingering on her aerobically perfect body. I'm human, I noticed. She's a person who cares what she looks like. She wants you to notice. Every week so far, she has worn a different pair of über expensive-looking shoes and they are always unscuffed, brand-new. They look like they are handmade from the skin of baby peacocks by elderly Italian artisans. They look like they've been soled with the hide of an embryonic rhino or a shark who swam into the wrong line at the wrong time. They are so delicate that I want to grab one from her foot, I want to twist it in my hands and feel it being destroyed.

I hate her for that, for making me feel that way. It feels disgusting. *I* feel disgusting.

And for her, I have to miss basketball practice, which used to be the best part of my day. But you know what? Screw it, because I quit.

I'm going to quit everything that I *can* quit.

I can't quit school because it would give Mom too much to grieve, but right now I feel like I would if I could.

I look across the street to the spot where he'd normally be waiting for me, smoking, shirt untucked, looking *insouciant*, which is exactly the kind of word he loved.

And there she is.

Ms. Daffodil Blue, age seventeen.

She sees me. Yeah, well, I quit her, too. I already have, but right now, in this second, I know that I have to make it official, I just don't know how. So I do the only thing I can do, which is run. She yells, "Wait, you jerk! Sharky, wait for me."

But I *can't*.

I jump over a garbage can to avoid a crowd of little kids on their way to the playground. I sprint. When I don't see her behind me, I stop and type, *Arrête*. And the word flies into her pocket, fast and low, like a weapon swinging and hitting, spinning her right out of the neighborhood. I run again. I haven't run like this for ages, glancing off surfaces, climbing things, jumping gaps. I run so hard and so fast that I can't feel my feet on the ground anymore, I'm flying, I'm soaring.

I'm a pigeon, swooping high and far.

I'm flying.

All I need now is a Nimbus 2000, and I'd be out of here for good.

Last Halloween we went to the party as Harry Potter, Ron, and Hermione.

Daff was Harry. I was Ron. There are pictures of us howling with laughter on Facebook, the three of us, The King's face crumpling so hard that his eyes vanish into the folds of his cheeks and he looks so happy and he looks so young and weird and crazy and his hair is hidden under his Hermione wig and he's laughing, and he's everything he was and wasn't at the same time.

That's the picture that *People* magazine used when they ran his obit.

That's the one everyone thinks was really him, mouth open, eyes rolling, wearing a girl's uniform from Hogwarts, looking like an idiot.

They have no idea who he was. They have no idea who he could have been.

Harry Potter fan, they said. Like that was something sordid. Come on. Everyone liked those books when they were kids. The costumes were a joke and the media made too much of everything, that's a fact.

I'm standing on top of a chain-link fence. I have no idea how I got here. I stop to breathe, my heart hammering. Someone yells,

"Hey, kid!" and I am going again and running down an alley like a guy who has stolen a purse and can't be stopped, not now. Not ever.

My phone buzzes.

U can't run 4evr, she texts.

Pls, she texts. *I'm gng 2 puke.*

I run faster and faster and my heart beats out the words, *I quit you, I quit you, I quit you.* I run light and hard, people staring, wondering if they should stop me, looking for the nonexistent purse under my arm, searching for blood on my hands. They're confused by my uniform, my tie and white shirt. Should they do something? They are all too well dressed and too dazed, actors playing the part of fancy New Yorkers who don't know what to do with this interruption in their regular scene.

No one does anything. Because that's what people are like. That's what they do, which is to say, they *don't.* They wait for someone else to solve the problem, fix the leak, stop the end from coming.

They don't *do* anything.

I *am* running from something I've done. I'll be running from it forever, but I'll never be able to get away.

That's how it works. You can't quit your past. That's just how it is when your best friend is dead and your other (newly former) best friend is chasing you through the streets of Manhattan, sweat streaming down both of your faces, not knowing how it's ever going to end or if it can. Because all I really want is for her to catch up to me. All I really want is for her to hold on to me tight.

THEN IT'S THE LAST DAY OF CLASSES. DID I TAKE EXAMS?
Did I pass?

Do I care?

The grief counselor wears pale pink suede sandals with three-inch heels that look like they've been dipped in actual gold. A newborn lamb died for those, I bet. A fetal pig. Something small and pink. Her toenails are painted like the Fabergé eggs that Daff's mom collects. Her calf muscles look like they were carved out of soft stone. "You're doing fine," she tells me. "You are going to be fine. Keep this." She presses a crystal into my palm so hard that it hurts.

I nod mutely. My palm feels bruised. The first thing I will do with this crystal is throw it as far and as hard as I can.

"You may want to start talking again," she says. "You may find you have something to say."

I nod. Shrug. Try to arrange my face appropriately.

"Okay," she says. "Okay." She gives me a pat on the shoulder.

Pat, pat, pat. I feel like I'm something that she's efficiently checking off her list. I stare at her.

"You can go," she says. "You're done."

Then I'm free. That's it. My shoes squeaking on the hallway floor. The bang of lockers. Filling my bag with crumpled papers and textbooks that I don't know what else to do with. Teachers leaning in doorways, looking depleted. People whooping and tumbling into each other like suddenly they take up too much room to be contained in this building, like they are bursting to be gone. There are ties all over the floor because that's a thing that happens on the last day, you take off your tie and throw it.

I wonder what happens to those ties. Each one costs forty-nine dollars at the school uniform store. I keep mine on. When no one is looking, I scoop a few extras from behind the trash. I'm always losing my stupid tie.

"Dude, have a good one, see you." "Catchya after break." "Smell ya next year." "Text me if you wanna . . ." Words thrown over their shoulders so they won't see my face or have to wait for an answer. I stare at them so hard they disappear, whisper thin, until I can see past them, through to the wall, then through the wall, outside, past buildings and cars and sidewalks on the other side to The King's gravestone and then I think, Get over it, you sick maudlin freak, you need to just get over it.

From a distance, I see Daff dumping her books into a garbage can, her tie tied around her hair like a bandanna.

There once was a blue girl named Daff / Who made the Sharkboy laugh / She rode on the train / To protect her hair from the rain / Because she hates when her hair looks like crap. I can't explain Daff except to say that when I see her, it's not like a magnet pulling me toward her, it's something so much more powerful than that. I want to be close to her. I need to be close to her. I would kill to make her laugh. I want to ride down the railing at her building on my board. I need her to get excited about something she's listening to and reach over without warning and jam her earbud into my ear. I want her and me and The King to grab some falafel and go to the place in the park where there's a cave, an actual cave, and to eat them there, even though it stinks like a drunk's piss. I need to touch the skin of her shoulder with my tongue.

I hate that I still want her.

I hate that I still love her.

I want to not think about the funeral every time I see her.

I want to not think about how weird she looked, like someone who was not Daff dressed up as Daff. Her overly made-up red lips, her fake tears, her look-at-me pose, the way she smiled just slightly at the cameras, the way she knew they loved her.

Don't think about the funeral. Don't think about the funeral. Don't think about the funeral. Don't—

And then, *bam*, like the time travel machine that Mrs. S. will never have access to, I am hurled back in time to the church and there I am in that cold stone room, the light filtering through the stained glass splashing inappropriately beautiful rainbows in patterns on the pews. The oppressive presence of a God that The King didn't even believe in is everywhere, from the worn leather on the kneeling bench to the oily marks on the backs of the benches from people pressing their foreheads there. I couldn't sit, so I stood in an aisle. My legs wouldn't bend.

"Are you . . . ?" Daff had said, hesitating, her hand hovering near her face. I wanted to touch her face so bad. But I couldn't. My arms were paralyzed. ". . . okay?" Then she'd lifted her hair back, winding it up behind her head, knotting it into a bun. Everything she did looked like she was performing it. Her dress was dark red, something expensive from a movie that was black-and-white. "I mean, are you going to be okay? Obviously not. But. Why didn't you call me?" Her hand on my arm, her hand on my arm, her hand on my arm. *I love you,* I wanted to say, but didn't. I didn't say anything. I shook her arm off. In the pew beside me, Number Six was crying for real, her shoulders shaking, making a strangling sound. In front of her, Number Seven's lips were set in a straight line, as flat as a tabletop. She was, for some reason, staring at me. The King's dad looked stoically through me and Daff. His eyes drifting away from everyone's face.

Stoic was all wrong for this occasion. Monster.

"*D'accord. Je suis désolé,*" I whispered into Daff's perfect ear, the last of my voice feathering the air like tiny wings. I could smell apples.

"Everything totally sounds better in French," she said, like we were still friends, agreeing about something. "*Desolated.* It's a way better word than sorry."

My legs suddenly remembered how to move and I turned and ran, pushing people out of my way. Old people, young people, famous people, whoever. Daff yelled something, but I don't know what it was. Then I was outside. Throwing up. On the steps. Running the gauntlet of cameras and gawkers.

Then I left.

I walked to the Broadway-Lafayette station, down those stairs, down deeper and deeper and deeper than any grave, wishing the station would collapse above me and squash me, bury me in the rubble of everything I was doing wrong. When I finally got on the train, it was empty except for a group of old men playing some kind of flutes, the music of that so thin and delicate that I wanted to claw off my own ears. I didn't need that. I needed something angrier. Something with drums and a guitar solo that tore through your skin. The train broke down like it always does at the worst times and I was trapped. I sat there for an hour, that flute music wrapping around me in thin threads like a cobweb, while somewhere in Manhattan, people (and Daff) sang hymns around The King's coffin and pretended not to be scanning the crowd for famous faces that they could whisper about afterward on the Internet.

I missed the funeral. My best friend's funeral. What kind of person does that?

I do. I guess I'm a worse person than his dad, after all. *I'm* the bad guy.

I did it.

It was me.

10

I PACK MY STUFF TO TAKE TO MY DAD'S: T-SHIRTS. SHORTS.
Trunks. Hoodies. I don't know what I'll need. I don't care. I throw in
some flip-flops and a pair of boots. It's cold in Canada, right? I've
seen pictures that Dad has sent of the island where he lives. It
looks shadowy and treed and like it possibly never stops raining,
like even the air is wet. The ocean is a cold green-gray. His photos
never have people in them. It's almost as if he lives on a different
planet, a place where no one exists. I stuff in the sweater that Daff
knitted and a pair of too-small kicks and a few extra T-shirts that
aren't quite clean, but good enough, including my favorite that
says, *I ♥ nuns*, which was funny only to me, Daff, and The King.
Mom throws me a bag containing sunscreen and kid medicine,
like Benadryl and After Bite. Granola bars. Vitamins shaped like
gummy bears.

"Here," she says. "Got some stuff you'd probably forget."

I stare at her, bewildered.

"It's all they had," she says, defensively. "Your dad might not have this kind of thing. I think there aren't any . . . stores."

She suddenly hiccups and then starts to cry the kind of tears you cry when you're pretending not to be crying. She looks confused, like this wasn't her decision, or maybe like she didn't notice that I am not a little boy anymore, wearing imaginary red boots, staring out to sea. She has dyed her hair a light mauve in preparation for her trip. It makes her look older, grayer, more tired. Or maybe she is just older, grayer, and more tired.

"I'm going to cut your hair," she says suddenly. "It's so shaggy. Can I cut it?"

I hesitate, then nod.

I follow her into the kitchen and I sit at the table and stare at the clock on the microwave. I wonder how many times I have sat exactly here while she cut my hair, how I've somehow gone from being a kid to being me all under the flashing blades of her scissors. The clock glows green. The microwave hasn't changed. Nothing is changed except the colors. I wish I had a time-lapse image of our kitchen, of the layers Mom has added, covering up each and every mistake. Every new boyfriend she had, once he left, the kitchen would change. Every new job. Every new thing. I wonder if I could take a lesson from that somehow. Just add more layers and more layers until the paint covering me would be so thick it would be armor. The clock blinks. The scissors cleave my hairs into pieces. The time always seems to change while I'm blinking. She cuts and cuts and cuts, the sound of my hair being sliced cuts through me and makes me want to cry like the kid I used to be, sitting here, doing this. She paints the ends with bleach, so that it looks like my head is glowing gold. But bleach isn't like paint. Bleach doesn't add a layer, it takes one away, leaving that hair more exposed than it was before. Like how I feel when I see Daff.

Revealed, somehow. Too seen.

So I won't see her.

I'm just trying to explain it to myself, you know.

I lie on my bed when Mom is done and I smell the chlorinated smell of my own head, and I watch *Sharkwater* over and over again, all night. I've watched it so much, it's like now I can remember actually doing the stuff that I'm seeing. The lines are blurred and blurred and gone. She's made my hair look even more like his. Now we're twins, clones, the same person and I'm the one who was diving with the sharks. I was releasing sharks from long lines. *I* was the hero.

I think when I'm old, I'll forget entirely that it actually wasn't me. And probably no one will know the difference.

Sharkboy.

Sharky.

Great White Me.

11

AMERICA IS A MONOTONY OF LAND PUNCTUATED BY SHARP
mountain ranges far below the plane that is hurtling me north and
west. I don't think I ever realized how meaningless everything looks
when it's small. How dry and tiny and squared off.

Just looking at the barren wasteland makes me crave water, a
tall glass with ice cubes, not this plastic cup of warm toxins in
front of me on the fold-out table that presses down on my knees.
The lakes and rivers out the window are shrinking veins. The towns
and cities are small tumors.

It's so easy to hate it from up here.

Then a blanket of clouds erases everything and I sit back in my
chair and try hard not to think.

I heard someone say that flying was a suspension of disbelief
and I guess it really is. If this metal tube weighing thousands of
pounds can stay up, why couldn't one kid fly?

I think of how his shirt billowed, wanting to inflate.

I turn my phone back on and it buzzes.

Daff: *R U GONE?*

Daff: *F U. SRSLY. F U.*

Daff: *MISS U. <3*

Daff: *TXT ME.*

Daff: *Pls.*

Delete, Delete, Delete. Delete all. *Je t'aime, Daffodil Blue. Au revoir. Je ne regrette rien. Je regrette tout. Je wish I had been paying enough attention in Français class to dit what I really mean. I wish I had been paying enough attention in French class to know why I'm doing this. Je ne sais pas. Je sais rien.*

I text The King instead: *Have a great summer, man. See ya in the fall. Catch ya on the flip side. Smell ya in September. Dude, text me if you wanna hang out.* Send, Send, Send, Send, Send. A flock of pigeons breaking free of the plane and soaring on the exhaust back to the East Coast, taking all my meaningless words with them to dissolve on a screen that is buried in a freaking coffin under the ground and what is wrong with me? What?

I take a photo out the window and filter it through so many filters that it just looks like a brown-tinted blur, crosshatched with tiny lines. Send again, because why not? A picture of my kicks. A shot of the aisle. A picture of the crappy cup of water. I can't stop. I am sending and sending and sending. I can picture the grass that must now be growing on his grave, vibrant and lush, sprinkled on the hour by a fancy irrigation system, vibrating with every notification on his phone even while his body is *decomposing*, which is a word that is dead leaves in my mouth, thick and fetid and brown, and, after all, how can anyone breathe in this tin can? The taste in my mouth is foul compost because I am rotting from the inside out because we both died that day because I deserve to die too because of what I did and because of what he saw and Daff. Daff. Daff.

Seriously, *stop*.

I can't make it stop.

The look on his face when he came leaping up the stairs of her brownstone, flinging open the door, and saw us. And she had just said, "Sharky," in a voice that meant that something was going to happen and my hands were in her hair in her hair in her hair and her face and my face and neither of us had been drinking and we were going to . . . It was going to happen and before he barged in, shattering the air like so much glass, like he'd stomped on something crystal with heavy shoes on. And he'd gone, "Whoa!" And we'd jumped apart, guilty, but for what? Nothing, nothing, nothing happened.

But his face. I mean, I don't know. I didn't know. He was . . .

It was a face you didn't forget, then I knew.

I got it.

He loved her, I guess.

He loved her and I got her.

But now neither of us does, so I hope he's happy wherever he is, I hope he knows that nothing will ever work now, ever again, between me and her. Or me and him. Or him and her.

It's all gone away, as soon as he let go, and his shirt

billowed

and he

tipped.

I start to cry hard, finally, and for real. My shoulders are shaking in a way that would be totally embarrassing if I cared. But

I don't care. I can't stop. It's like somehow something inside me has come unplugged and there's nothing that could stop it and I am hemorrhaging snotty tears everywhere. I won't stop, maybe not ever. Not for the older businessguy who angles his body away from me in the next seat. Not for the fake concern of the flight attendant. Not for anyone. Not for anything.

But when we touch down, I do.

I stop.

I am empty. Lighter.

Different.

I expect to look down at my hands and see feathers, ready to push me upward and away from here. But my hand is still my hand. And now I'm in Canada.

I am still me. Just me, for the first time in so long, I can't remember. Inhabiting me, I guess, is what I mean. I'm not Sharky The King Daff. I'm not one of three. Or, then, one of two. Or gone, zeroed out.

I'm here.

And when I walk to the baggage claim and wait for my bag to drop down onto the belt I feel like something inside me has been shaken free.

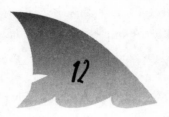

12

A CAR PULLS UP IN THE ROUNDABOUT IN FRONT OF THE airport. This Canadian air feels thinner and somehow smaller than the air at home, like even the molecules of oxygen are more compact and more polite, not big sprawling stinky American air. It smells like sleep breath and the threat of a storm, something crackling behind something else.

The car is purple and makes a sound like a gray whale singing for a mate. Which is great and majestic if you're a whale, but not so good for an old station wagon. Underneath the peeling purple paint are patches of green, brown, and rust that look like bad camo gear. I had no idea that people really drove cars like this. It looks like something from a movie about hillbillies, something that is nothing to do with me.

Shame crawls around under my skin like an army of caterpillars with sticky feet. It's a good thing I'm not talking because I don't have to decide what to say. Hello, hi, *hey there*. And there are no names for him that fit: JC Sr.? Papa? Dad? Father? Sir? Yeah, right.

Dad is about the furthest thing from a "sir" you could ever imagine. He's a "hey, dude" at best.

The King's dad is a "sir." He commands it. The way he moves into a room. The way his smile crawls into place with a slow deliberation that puts you in your place. My dad doesn't smile. Dad is a *grinner*.

The word PEACE is painted in gold sparkly paint in letters about a foot high across the rear door of the purple car, like it's been graffitied by a band of wayward hippies. The sight of that word and the way it is crooked lets me know all I need to know about my dad's so-called life, which involves caretaking a stopped-in-progress hotel building site on an island with nothing else on it.

No roads.

No stores.

No residents.

No one.

Nothing but trees and whatever animals lurk in their shadows. Deer, I guess. Probably rats.

Dad's "career" involves running off kayakers and campers to protect the property from fire and vandalism. For that, he gets paid in room and board and who knows what else, and he buys time to write his painfully crappy novels that he self-publishes and makes enough money from to send Mom a check for fifty dollars once a month. Impressive my dad is not.

My phone buzzes. Daff.

I type *Arrête* without reading what she wrote.

I add, *Au revoir.*

Why doesn't she get it? Why don't *I* get it?

I am quickly running out of French. Pretty soon I'll be reduced to saying, *Where is the library?* and *Please pass me a pen.* Or *Can you show me the way to the metro?*

The car grinds to a stop, then revs up, chokes, and goes again, circling. Sweat drips down my face and into my shirt, which is good because it disguises the wet patches I made when I was crying, but sucks because I stink. I'm guessing a washer and dryer are not things he has, and I know for sure there is no Laundromat.

The purple car circles me.

And circles me.

And circles me.

I am prey, with nowhere to go. Pretty much stunned into submission, unable to surface to get a breath of air. I only hope that it doesn't hurt too much when it finally bites.

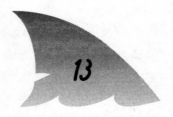

13

I HAVE ONLY EVER SEEN MY DAD WHEN HE COMES TO Brooklyn to visit me, which he does because that's what the judge said he has to do and not because he wants to do it, which is painfully obvious whenever it has happened. *Awkward* is stuck on him like a cobweb he walked into by mistake, covering his face and hands and everything he says. He takes me places I hate and fills up the space around us with a bunch of joviality and *trying*: baseball games and the Empire State Building and the freaking zoo, like he didn't get any updates when the calendar flipped over each year and I went ahead and got older and older and older and older and I hate baseball and I think zoos should be illegal and the Empire State Building?

Well, it's boring.

Sorry, but it is.

The elevator in the Empire State Building smells like hospitals. The view is something you've seen in pictures so many times that when you actually see it, it feels old already, like you're watching a rerun on TV. Unless you're my dad, and then you're snapping pictures like no one will ever go up there again, like no one would ever see *this*.

Last time he was in town, he took me and The King and Daff to a "fancy" dinner. We ended up at TGI Fridays on Forty-Second, uncomfortably making conversation over plates full of terrible shrimp, The King and Daff shooting looks at each other over the rims of their Shirley Temples. I tried to pretend it was so lame that it was actually cool. Ironic. But no one was buying what I was selling and Dad was trying too hard. Like always. Afterward, I seriously considered just drowning myself in the East River so that I'd never have to go through anything like that again. But I went along with it because after that it was all, oh, it's lunchtime, who wants a formal shrimp plate? Shall we take the town car to TGIs? Hmmm? Oh, that isn't funny? No, it isn't? Want to call your dad? He'll wear his fanciest T-shirt! Not funny? *Oh, okay.*

But I'd laugh because yeah, it was really at the expense of my dad, not me, and my friends got me. They knew what my dad was like. "You know," Daff whispered behind her menu, "your dad is kind of like a visitor from another planet. I feel like a scientist, observing life on Mars. Let us take notes." And just then, my dad stood up to go to the washroom and a server walked right into him with a tray of sizzling meat and Dad's legs were scalded and he kept saying, "Man, I am so sorry," while the waiter said things like, "Yeah? Well, maybe I'll sue you, jerk," and Dad apologized again and again as if he was a dog, which is what he reminds me of, specifically a golden retriever, he would have been wagging his tail exuberantly and knocking over more things in his effort to be forgiven. The King said, "I am a lawyer. I am a lawyer." And Daff laughed and laughed and actually, so did I, and it was only actually just now that I realized that Dad wasn't really the jerk in that situation.

It's better not to remember stuff.

It's better to just focus on the now. Buddhism 101. Or, you know, what I think Buddhism is. I was never into that stuff. That was The King's thing and who knows how much he made up and how much was real, how much was the philosophy of The King and how much was ancient religious tenets that could change everything if only we would just get on with it and believe in love and hope and peace and not attaching to anything ever. Not attaching to anyone. Not putting your hands into a girl's hair while your best friend's eyes see you and his face sees you and his heart sees you and just for a split second, his face is lightning-split open and you can see his brokenness. But you can also see her lips, right there and you didn't kiss them but you could have. You should have. And if the timing was just a few seconds the other way, you would have. And you are such a jerk for thinking that because then he would have seen something even worse.

But then again, why did he get to decide?

The purple car, look at it. I look at the purple car. I am not at Daff's place, she is not here, The King is not breaking. I am here and I am breathing and that's over and I don't have to think about how even looking at Daff gives me panic attacks so intense that I feel like my heart is rolling on a tsunami and one day it will rip right out of my chest like an alien baby and anyway thinking about her makes it hard to breathe this tiny, peculiar Canadian air.

I concentrate on the car, but I still can't seem to move or wave.

Instead, I let the time stretch and yawn between us, between me and Dad and his purple behemoth. Finally, he struggles out of the car through the window in a ridiculous painful-to-watch way, butt first.

Seriously.

I am incredulous, I type to The King. *Incredulity rules the day.*

"Yo, JC!" Dad shouts, half-in, half-out. Then he's out. "I mean, Shark Dude! Or Sharkboy! Yeah, Shark*boy*, right? Right," he answers himself, crossing those twelve feet between us in about three leaping, loping strides. His face has new wrinkles, spraying out from his eyes like his eyeballs were dropped into his head from such a great distance that they made splash marks in his flesh. His stubbly beard is gray.

When did he get so old?

He's bouncing on his feet like a runner waiting for a light to change. The grin flashes on and off his face like one of the neon signs advertising GIRLS GIRLS GIRLS near Times Square.

"Hey," he says. "Heyyyy." He holds out his hand. There's a tattoo on his wrist that says, *Writers write*. It looks itchy. He smells weird, if by "weird," I mean, "like someone who badly needs a shower," which I guess is how I'm going to spend the summer smelling, myself. Smelling good is sort of important to me. Or it was. Maybe it isn't anymore. Maybe I don't care.

"How was your flight? Was it good? Was there food? There's never food. I wondered . . . I mean, I worried . . ." He trails off, squints at me like he can barely make me out. "I've been at Costco. Stocking up. I hope you like . . . cereal. And chips."

I shrug. Everyone in the world likes cereal.

"What's your favorite? I didn't know so I bought . . ."

I know that Mom told him that I've stopped talking. I can tell he thought he'd be the miracle that would make me utter words again. Like now I'm going to say, "Cornflakes," or whatever, just to make him the winner. Well, screw that. Also, all cereal is the same. It's fine. It's good. Whatever. Seriously.

"It will pass," I'd heard Mom tell him. "Don't push him, John, okay? Leave him to sort it out."

When they were together, she used to get so mad at him. She'd start out nice, trying hard not to lose her temper, but you could see it crackling there, right behind her eyes. He'd be goofy and dumb and she'd be trying to say or do something important, and by the end, she'd be throwing things: glasses, shoes, a paperweight.

And he'd stand there grinning like a simpleton. Wagging.

Like now.

I put my sunglasses on.

The dads of the kids in my class do important stuff, like surgically repair cleft lips on orphans in Africa. Or they are philanthropists, pouring millions into finding a cure for breast cancer or tapeworm or whatever, or they at least own boutiques or grocery chains or star in crappy action films while running around with starlets. McFatty's dad is dead but everyone else has one, usually on wife number two or three or four. Rich guys, man. They'd make you sick, if you knew. But poor guys are equally bad, just in different ways. They aren't nobler or inherently better people, they are the same stupid idiots, but with less money. I wonder if it's necessarily true that all boys grow up to be disappointing men. I can't actually think of a single adult man I know who is a decent person. Not one.

"So," says Dad. "So, so, so . . . hey." He cocks his head. "Think you'll start talking again soon? 'Cause I've gotta be honest, this is tough. Talking to you and having you not answer. I feel weird about it. Man."

I shrug.

"I really want you to talk to me," he says. "About everything. Anything. I want to be here for you. It's going to be tough if you won't tell me what's going on. Look, I know it's your decision. Everything's a decision. But I . . . want to help."

Right.

Sure.

The truth is that Dad wants me to talk so he can validate his own role in my life. He can be all heroic and like, I'M LISTENING TO YOU BECAUSE I'M SUCH A GOOD DAD, LOOK AT ME! LISTENING! HURRAY FOR ME! His need for my voice is like a vibration on a guitar string, quivering between us. If I could, I would reach out and twang that string. Snap it between my fingers. My silence is unbelievable to him, like he's so *shocked* that his declaration didn't make me suddenly start pouring out my heart and soul. My silence makes him louder and louder, like he can make up for my silence with all-caps-level volume.

"OKAY. SO I GET IT," he says. "I'M A BIG BOY AND I CAN WAIT. YOU'VE GOT YOUR STUFF. YOU GOTTA DEAL. IT'S OKAY. SO *I'LL* TALK. LET'S SEE. WEATHER? BEEN SUPER HOT, OF COURSE WATER IS RATIONED AND THE GRASS IS ALL DEAD HERE BECAUSE WHO CARES ANYWAY BECAUSE THAT'S NATURE, RIGHT? THERE AREN'T LAWNS ON THE ISLAND. IT'S NOT THAT KIND OF PLACE.

SUBURBIA, ICK. YOU'LL LOVE IT THERE, ON THE ISLAND, BECAUSE IT'S QUIET. UNTOUCHED. LIKE HOW THE WORLD SHOULD BE. I LIKE QUIET. YOU'LL SEE. YOU MUST, TOO, RIGHT? HA HA. BUT WOW, YOU MUST BE GLAD TO BE HERE, OFF THAT PLANE, AWAY FROM NEW YORK AND EVERYTHING, WELL . . . THIS MUST FEEL LIKE A DIFFERENT PLANET, HUH."

Shut up, I want to say. *Just shut up. Please shut up.*

He grins and bounces and stares at me. I hold up my hand in the universal sign of *seriously, stop now.*

"You could tell me to shut up," he says finally. "But I guess not. Not yet anyway. We should get going. But it's so good to see you. It's so *good.*" He takes a lurching step toward me and there it is: the hug. My skin shivers with revulsion. If I had a superpower, I'd like for it to be awkwardness repulsivity. I'd be like a reverse magnet. Anything awkward wouldn't even be able to get close. I smile a tiny bit, then stop, hoping he didn't see that.

I don't smile.

I stopped smiling.

I will never smile again.

Why was I smiling? It wasn't even funny.

My best friend is dead.

Hey, here's a joke, self! What do you get when you fall off the forty-second floor? Answer: dead! *Bad um cha!*

Not funny, no? Too soon?

I pick up my bag and move toward the car, not looking at him. I don't know what happens next, but I guess Dad's puppy-legs wound around each other, tripping him up, because suddenly he's lying facedown on the sidewalk and blood is dripping from his nose as he pushes himself back up, looking dazed. I blink hard because *bam* out of nowhere, I'm right back there, on Eleventh and Fifty-Third and the blood on the sidewalk the blood on the sidewalk the blood on the sidewalk the blood.

It's nothing the same.

Why do I think it's anything like something that is the same?

Dad gets to his feet and there is blood gushing down his lip, which he licks. I look away. He says, "I can't believe that happened." He half laughs. "First day, new feet." He points at his sandals, which look like something a German tourist would go crazy over. You can always tell the German tourists in the city by those dumb shoes and none of them are tripping over their own feet. I shrug in a way that is meant to communicate everything: *You're a loser. You're clumsy. I hate you. I don't know you. I don't want to be here.* You know, all of that.

Dad wrenches the passenger door open and finds a filthy-looking tissue on the seat and stuffs it up his nose. "There," he says. "Better." Which sounds like "bedder." There is blood on his stupid hipster stubbly beard and his stupid inside-out, probably ironic T-shirt.

"By dose hurds," he says. "Shood."

I take my phone out of my pocket, switch it over to my photo app and take a picture of him, filtered to look like an old Polaroid, the photo even more hipster than the hipster himself. I send the picture to Mom. I type, *Dad's here.*

Swooop.

Let her look at that.

Let her see what she's done to me.

14

OUTSIDE THE CAR WINDOW, FIELDS BECOME A TOWN AND then become fields again and forests. I feel carsick. I miss the stupid F train and even the overcrowding and stench of the 6. If I try hard enough, I could even miss the bus. "Everything is a decision," Daff said. "You can decide how much pain to feel." I press a point on my wrist and believe that it works. The car heaves back and forth. Daff was always right and always wrong and I have to stop thinking about her, but she's in my head and I can't get her out, like a song that won't leave me alone.

Dad talks and weaves between lanes. Maybe he thinks if he doesn't hurry the island won't still be there when the car stops. I guess the ferry could leave without us. I kind of hope it will. Even *this* place looks like a smaller town than I've ever seen and we are going away from it? To an . . . island? It seems so crazy. Absurd. And every other SAT synonym for *stupid* that you can think of: *vacuous, vapid, daft*. The whole escapade is something you'd see in a sitcom and you wouldn't understand how things connected until the misunderstanding was cleared up in the last scene or until you just stopped caring and changed the channel.

Except it's real.

It's my summer.

Well, yippee for me.

I close my eyes. Closing your eyes when you are mute is like shutting the blinds on your office door. It says, *Thank you for stopping by, but I am currently unavailable.* A message that Dad does not receive, evidently.

". . . and I make extra money with the scallops. Selling them. I have a friend who is doing it, too. Really lucrative. You'd be surprised. I mean, I didn't think I'd like doing that, but you know, a guy has to make money and HEY, LOOK AT THAT, AN EAGLE? Bald eagle. I've never seen one in America, but here they are everywhere. Ironic, right? Amazing birds. Take some pictures and wow your friends when you get home. Seeing them never gets old and . . ."

I want to reach up and peel off my ears so that the silence inside me and the silence around me can find each other. I make a show of leaning back in the seat and sighing deeply, like I'm about to nod off. *The office is closed, Dad. God, would you shut up already?*

The King's dad had an office that took up a whole floor of their apartment, which wasn't even one apartment, it was four that had been ingeniously attached together to make one massive space. He did not have the kind of office with blinds. His office had push-button everything, shades that opened and closed with a muffled hush like a footfall in thick carpet. Everything in his rooms was like that. Even the bathroom had air as soft and fresh as golf-course grass. In fact, there was actually a real flat square of grass on the counter that he trimmed with nail scissors. He could tell if one blade was out of place. He hated it when we touched it, but it was impossible not to do it. Impossible not to lay your hand flat there and see the outline of your fingers pressed into that rich man's golf green.

The grass didn't fit him. Not at all. A bathroom that would fit The King's dad would be made of jagged rock and broken things, ice, and steel blades.

The King's dad was neither fresh nor hushed.

The grass was another test that we failed again and again so he could hate us more. There was probably a reason for that, right? Like maybe he was locked in the attic when he was a kid. Maybe he was beaten with snakes. Or maybe he's just the worst person who ever lived.

I'm guessing it's the latter, but what do I know?

It's not like he ever discussed his past.

The stuff he said was either a criticism or a decree. Every time he talked, it sounded like he was hurtling down a slope, a pile of something inevitable crashing down, smashing the listener to smithereens. He'd had so much plastic surgery that his face moved wrong with his voice, making him seem even less real, both ancient and ageless. Like a *being* rather than a person. Like something you couldn't quite put into a category. Feelingless, but alive.

A monster.

Zen, baby, that's what The King would say to him, in this sing-song voice that wasn't his, either. *Find your Zen, Big Daddy.*

His dad would yell, spittle flying, and The King would smile his own version of that small, slow smile. The power smile. They would smile at each other, in slow-motion like that, seeing who would win, teeth against teeth. It made me think of the goblin shark, the ugliest shark in the world, the shark that can actually throw its own mouth outward from its body, surprising its prey. The shark whose smile is pretty much always fatal.

Zen, baby.

The King had his own philosophy. One day, he was going to write it down. It was like Buddhism, basically, he said. But better. Buddhism without the hippie angle, the flowing rivers and things people couldn't relate to anymore, living in New York City. It was about how you could skim along the surface of life or you could really live it, but you could do it without letting other people get to you because you would not attach to other people. Wrap yourself in a veneer that disguised you and confused other people. Save the inner warmth of your true spirit for a chosen two. His Buddhism had sidewalks with rivers running underneath, you just had to believe they were there. Cold, clear rivers that led to the sea.

Daff and I were his two.

Daff and The King were mine.

I can't explain it like he did. It sounded right when he said it. Ideal. Perfect. And most of all, correct. Save your humanity for the humans, he said. Give everyone else an automaton who meets their expectations. Never let anyone down. Remember the river is there, even when you can't see it.

His dad thought he was ridiculous. A *fucking idiot.* And he didn't hesitate to say it. *Hey, have you met my fucking idiot son?* he'd say to his cronies and then he'd laugh, and they'd laugh, because that's what he was like. They'd be uncomfortable because, seriously, who says that about your own kid, in front of your own kid. But they'd laugh because he was a guy whose laugh commanded your own laugh out of you, even when nothing was funny.

Especially when nothing was funny.

I'd say that his dad was the *fucking idiot* but no one asked me and no one would dare say that about that man, even though they all probably privately thought it.

Fucking idiot, he'd say, and The King would cringe down inside his cool veneer and smile slower and slower and slower, his feet feeling through the ground for that river that wasn't even there.

I run my finger along a vinyl seam on the seat. My nails are too long.

I think about The King's nails, growing, in his marble box.

Was there anything left of his fingers?

He used to get manicures. Mom laughed when I told her, offered to buff my nails, but I said no. Embarrassed that I'd told her. Embarrassed for The King. Embarrassed for how different it all was, a bus and two trains away.

On the first day of school, me all pressed in my new white shirt, blue pants, plaid tie, blazer, feeling like a freak in a costume, the teacher said, "So we have a new kid. This new kid's name is John. John, come on up here and talk a whole bunch of bullshit lies about yourself or even the truth, if you're that way inclined."

The teachers at the Royal Pricks' Academy always swore. They thought it made them cutting edge. Different. Radical. When *really*, I wanted to tell them, the "Academy" was no different from Red Hook High. The only difference was the way the kids oozed the kind of laconic cool confidence that slid across the floor like oil and kept me slipping, never sure when I was okay, when I was safe to stand. They were all always playing a game, something with complicated rules that no one really understood but also would never admit to not understanding. A game that was more-than-slightly dangerous.

That's when I did my speech about the sharks and how they matter.

When I *cried*.

Fucking idiot, The King's dad would have said. *Look at you, blubbering up there, you fucking idiot faggot*. (He threw in *faggot* when he was feeling extra cruel.)

Afterward, I walked alone down the empty echoing hall to the bathroom. I remember feeling really tired, and not only because it took an hour and a half to get to the school and I'd come early, just to make sure. It was a different kind of tired. The kind of tired that you feel in the part of you that's nothing to do with your body, more like the universe had recently become too heavy to move around in. I held my hands under the cold tap and stared at myself, wondering how I came to be here and why, exactly, I was such a loser and what my old friends were doing at Red Hook and why I'd let my mom talk me into this weird alternate universe where I didn't belong.

Who *cries*?

I looked younger in a tie, like a kid playing dress up. I tightened the knot in the mirror so hard that I nearly choked.

Then The King came in. I jumped, not going to lie. He startled me. He let out a short laugh and then he lit a cigarette and drew on it in one long breath, let it out slowly in a twirling shape. He sat down next to me on the floor, the smoke ringing his head. He looked like a cartoon genie emerging from a bottle.

He said, "I think you take that movie a little too seriously, bro. I mean, it was a good film but everything is a lie. Everyone has an agenda. And no one's gonna die."

Well, eff you, you liar, I think now.

Someone *did* die, after all.

He did.

I swallow hard, carsickness and sadness congealing in my throat like sour milk. Cough into my hand.

Dad talks and talks. His voice isn't boulders, it's just annoying, like sand being flicked repeatedly in your face. He grinds on, grating on my last nerve.

I keep my eyes closed. I do what I've done since I was little and feeling anxious, do what was prescribed by some shrink in a completely nonhelpful "support group for anxious kids." What I do is I imagine my happy place. Which is underwater. In the sea.

I picture the sharks sliding through the blue depths.

I count the shark species, naming them all in my head.

Slower and slower and fewer and fewer and fewer of them until suddenly it's just entirely blue and I'm asleep and I'm dreaming that I'm underwater and I'm looking and looking and looking and there aren't any sharks and between me and the surface is only blood and I gasp and nearly wake up except suddenly I'm standing on the platform at the Smith-9th station looking down over the whole city, my uniform wearing me, turning me into someone different, someone who matters. A homeless dude laughs at me and throws something, a bottle of piss, which splashes my pants and I want to go home and change but then I'm back at school, at the bathroom sink and The King is there, crouched on the bathroom floor, which I think actually was marble, too (What is with rich people and marble? Don't they get it? That's what they make head-stones out of. That's the material of your grave.), going, "Guess you'll be called Sharkboy from now on, which if you think about it, is better than being called Freak. But me, I'm gonna call you Great White. Because you're white, see? And maybe you'll be great. Probably not though. Probably none of us will. But in movies, it's always the charity kid that comes out on top. So that's you. You get to be the underdog. A real-life heeeee-ro. Savin' everyone. Even maybe me." But because it's a dream, that's where it stops being real and where he turns around. And then I see the hole on his back and blood coming out and suddenly he has gills and he's flop-ping around on the floor and I can't save him and I can't save him and then I see that we're on the sidewalk and there is a stupid river, after all. I nudge him with my foot so he can flop into it, and even though he can't swim, the current takes him faster and faster and then he's out of sight and I'm crying instead of following. And then I wake up, sweat pouring from my face, and Dad is still *talking* like nothing has happened and I roll down the window and take great greedy gulps of air.

"OH MAN," says Dad. "WANT ME TO PULL OVER? ARE YOU GONNA PUKE?"

I shake my head no.

I breathe slowly.

I take out my phone and I text The King. *Dude,* I type. *I am so freaking sorry. I love you. I hope you found the river. Don't let anyone piss on your pants.* Then I delete it without sending it because even though he's dead, I don't want him to read that and I don't know why I don't and I don't know what I'm sorry for and the things that I don't know that I should are so big they are crushing me into the seat like too much gravity and for a minute I let myself sink, finless, drowning and . . .

"THE BOOG IS GOIG SO WELL! YOU HAB DO READ ID!" Dad suddenly shouts, snorting loudly to clear his nose. "IT HAS TIME TRAVEL. YOU CAN BE MY BETA READER! THAT'S THE GUY WHO READS IT FIRST. I'M IN ONE OF THOSE READING GROUPS ON THE INTERNET BUT I DON'T LET THEM SEE IT IN CASE THEY STEAL MY IDEA. MAYBE YOU CAN MAKE SOME NOTES FOR ME, LIKE ABOUT WHAT YOU KIDS SAY NOW, LIKE . . . NOOB." I stare at him in the mirror and shake my head at him but he isn't looking, he's watching the road. I like looking at his face when he isn't looking back. I feel like he's a mystery and if I solve him then I'll understand me. The mystery is how much of a buffoon he is, how round-edged and slow-witted. His face is mine, but older and softer. His beard and eyebrows are threaded with gray. The skin flakes around his nose. He rolls down the window and pays the woman in a booth. We're here. The ferry.

"Hey," he says out the window. "We make it?"

She nods, bored. "Lane thirty-two," she says flatly, like she's actually putting effort into layering each single syllable with ennui.

"Have a *great* day," Dad says, oblivious, turning his eyes to me in the mirror. "I know the kids say 'noob,' the kids at the beach say it all the time. You're going to have the best summer of your whole life. You love the ocean, right? Well, this island is . . . It's amazing. You'll die. I mean—" He hesitates. "Not, like, *die*. Bad choice of words, eh. God, I'm sorry, kid. That must have been . . ." He does look sorry, his eyes crinkling up until his face looks as puckered and weathered as a piece of fruit that's been left in the bowl for months too long. "I'm really sorry," he says again. I nod, to let him off the hook.

He looks a little too relieved.

"Anyway, maybe you can have some adventures for me to write about," he says. Then he laughs too hard—he's been eating potato chips like a starving man—and oily crumbs glisten around his mouth and are stuck between his teeth, like some kind of chip apocalypse.

"Chip?" he asks.

My stomach contracts. I shake my head no.

TIME TRAVEL, I type on my phone.

The phone accepts it.

The phone accepts everything.

Swoop, swoop.

15

SOMEHOW WHEN SOMETHING HAPPENS AND YOU CAN'T photograph it and send it somewhere, anywhere, it's the worst kind of loneliness.

I slap my phone against my leg, like that will revive the dead battery for long enough that I can take a picture. I want to show someone (Daff). I want to say, *Look at this*. I want someone (Daff) to say, *Wow*.

Because, seriously, this *place*. This is not what I was expecting. Not even a bit.

Mrs. S. would die. It puts the Keys to shame. It's freaking breathtaking.

"You can plug it in when we get to the cabin," says Dad. "The car charger thing is broken but I've hooked up batteries to solar panels up there and you can plug in anything. We're completely off the grid."

I give him a look that he misses entirely. I'm lucky my dad is not a genius. It's kind of like being parented by a cartoon. Everything about him is two-dimensional. There, but not there.

"Cool, eh?" he says. He gestures with his arm, a sweeping circle, like Mrs. S. waving down passersby to look at her display of fresh cod.

Yeah, I nod. I don't know who I'd want to see this more: Mrs. S.? Or Daff. (Daff, Daff, always Daff.)

It looks like a scene from a jigsaw puzzle or a postcard of somewhere that no longer exists, as though it really is TIME TRAVEL. The ferry weaves through islands that are dark-green-thick with forests, like cakes with too much icing, top-heavy. So many trees. The islands should sink into the sea from the weight of all that forest. I've never seen trees like this.

Or islands.

I've got to be honest. I didn't know places like this existed. You hear about deforestation and the raping of the rain forest and clear-cutting and how everything is wrecked, so I guess I just went ahead and believed it was too late. I guess I thought everything had been cut down and destroyed. Everything like this, that is.

When you live in a city, it can be hard to even know that other realities are out there.

Reality that's like this.

Nature in abundance.

I feel stupid even thinking that, but . . .

I reach for my phone to type *nature in abundance* before I remember that it's dead. And so is he.

Sailboats dot the waters with huge ballooning sails full of

wind. We pass an island with colorful tents splayed out down a hillside. Kayakers paddle near the shore in bright yellow and red boats that look like bathtub toys.

It's almost ridiculous, how pretty it is. It's pretend. It can't be real. But I know that it is because the air smells green and alive and salty and like forever would smell if it had a scent.

Then suddenly, amazingly (or not), I have an attack of feelings that are the opposite of what I should be feeling. I mean, shouldn't this kind of thing make you feel joy? If nothing else in the world makes you feel joy, this should. All this greenness. Well, this scene just suddenly and totally pisses me off. Like how dare it be so beautiful? The King is dead. I am so angry and sad and empty. I kick my foot against a huge bin labeled *Life Preservers* and my toes crunch in a satisfyingly painful way. Then my eyes tear up again and I put my sunglasses on and stare into the black reflection on my phone, keeping my eyes off everything that is alive and diamond-sparkling on the horizon against the backdrop of the too-blue summer sky.

16

THE CAR PULLS TO A STOP AT THE TOP OF A PUBLIC
dock. The road has narrowed and gravel crunches under the tires.
Dad swings the car up into a patch of dirt and grass that isn't quite
a parking spot. I have a feeling that parking lots aren't really a thing
here. You just . . . stop. The dock itself is a long, long, long ramp
leading to a small landing down a steep plank. It has a railing painted
bright red. At the distant end of it, an aluminum boat is bobbing in
the swell.

"Well," says Dad, "you might not talk, but you gotta work. We
have to carry this stuff"—he points—"down there." He unlocks
the back door and then has to use his whole body weight to pull it
open. The hinges groan reluctantly. "This car." He shakes his head.
"I wouldn't have one if I didn't need to move so much food. They're
so terrible for the whole world. Environment. Everything. And this
one, well. Piece of crap, really."

I nod. Can't disagree there. A hunk of rusty metal falls on the gravel from somewhere in the vicinity of the back door. "Yeah," he says. "Rusty."

I look at the boxes and bags that look like enough to last three summers: crates and cases and overflowing sacks of food. It takes an hour to drag it all down to the boat, the last part so alarmingly steep that my ankle remembers its injury and starts to throb. "Low tide," Dad says cryptically. Our bodies are aching and our skin is weeping sweat into our stinging eyes. The boat itself sinks lower and lower into the sea with each load. Up close, it looks questionably safe at best. Patches of rust splay out along its sides like it's been paintballed with the stuff. I don't know much about boats, but nothing about this one screams *seaworthy*. I wonder where Dad purchases his vehicles. The junkyard?

When we finally get going though, it seems okay. The cooler air off the water is such a relief that I'm not even sure I'd care if we sank. The motor vibrates noise around me. The ocean itself looks cold and clear and welcoming. My scalp prickles with sunburn.

The noise drowns out any possibility of talking, thank god, which means even Dad shuts up for a change. The life jacket Dad has forced me to put on is stretching my head away from my body, like those African tribesmen who use rings to lengthen their necks. The boat charges forward, slamming up and down on the waves, *whap whap whap*. Dad is smiling at the horizon. I stare at his profile in the mist of the spray that the boat is creating, pounding into the water like it is.

He's different here.

He's not the bumbling doofus he is in New York. It's like he fills the space differently. He looks okay, solid inside his own skin.

Under *this* sky. New York is like a T-shirt he's borrowed from someone else that is stretched out wrong and fits him badly and makes him always look like he wants to scratch at where the tag is rubbing his neck.

Here, he fits.

This is a fact. It doesn't make me like him any more or anything, it's just an observation.

The boat smashes down hard on the wake of a passing cruiser and a bunch of bananas fly out of a box and into the glass-green water. I think about reaching for them, but I don't. Instead, I trail my hand through the water, which is ice cold, spraying up my shirt and soaking me through. I feel for my phone in my pocket. Still there. I reach for it to take an Instagram of the bananas bobbing behind us, but the battery is still dead. The salt spray freckles the screen. I shove it back in my pocket.

It takes a half hour or maybe less until Dad slows the engine, and then he is nosing the boat onto the shore of a pebbled beach, the aluminum crunching hard against the rocks. He jumps off the bow and pulls the rope, shifting the whole boat from floating to grounded. The muscles in his arms ripple.

Above us, the face of a cabin peers down through the foliage like a shy kid. Reflecting in the late-afternoon light, the glass seems to appear and then disappear in the shadows. It's up a flight of steps that are made out of driftwood, oddly angled and steep. I think about the huge pile of boxes and bags in the boat and sigh.

No wonder Dad has muscles.

A dog barks from inside, followed by more barking, as though

Dad has the entire SPCA camped out in his living room. All around, the trees are making dappled shadows that splay over the pale pebbles of the beach, mottle the stairs, freckle the water.

It's so pretty. There is no explanation for why I feel like punching a tree trunk just to feel pain. I have to shove my hands in my pockets and will myself not to do that. Make myself feel less crazy. Is this what going crazy is like?

I have never seen trees like these. Some are squat and stunted in permanently bent positions, like the wind has blown them sideways and they never bothered to right themselves. Some are huge and obviously ancient, their bark so gnarled and twisted they make me think of the skin of old people, leathered and thick. The treetops vanish into the dusking sky. Looking up makes me dizzy. Scattered among them are smooth-skinned trees that look almost soft. Dark green waxy leaves, red papery bark feathering down to the ground in the wind.

"Arbutus," Dad says. I reach out and touch one and it feels firm and smooth, like cool human flesh. I pull back. Hands into pockets. Pretend not to be weirded out. Pretend not to be weird, in general, I guess.

"The boys are saying hello," Dad says. "Come on. Let's go up and let them out before they break through the glass door. We'll haul the stuff up in a few."

I follow him up the long stairs. He keeps a running description of everything we can see: types of trees, a passing bird. I wonder if there will be a test at the end.

"Salal," he says. "Dried seaweed we use as fertilizer. Douglas fir. Bald eagle." My legs feel funny, like they are someone else's

legs, which makes sense, because this is someone else's life. Someone else's forest. Someone else's crooked steps, grass and moss
growing on the rotting wood. Someone else's cabin, lopsided and
saggy.

But unfortunately not someone else's dad.

"It's not really a house," he says. "More of a cabin. Don't expect
much. I mean, *I* like it, but I get how it might be a shock to you,
city boy."

I pretend to not be shocked, but I guess he's right and I am.
Rustic doesn't even begin to cover it. I follow him inside, past the
front porch where a molding floral sofa sags depressingly toward
the boards. A hammock with an assortment of empty beer cans
scattered under it swings in a cold breeze. There is a table with
four typewriters in various states of disrepair: partially pulled apart
and rusty looking. Shells sit in rows along the balcony. A sign on
the door says, PLEASE COME IN, UNLESS THE DOOR IS LOCKED, IN
WHICH CASE, STAY THE ^*&! OUT.

Everything smells unfamiliar and wrong, that's the first thing
I notice. Not just the dog smell, but everything. And the dogs
themselves look like wolves, three of them, stepping on and over
one another to get to me and Dad, their ice-colored eyes fixed on
my face, fur bristling.

I can feel myself starting to scrunch up inside, anxious, like I
used to when Mom would take me to that group diligently once a
week to help me try to figure out why. The old feeling of panic
catches me off guard. I'm not much used to dogs. Not dogs like
these, dogs that look like they should be pulling sleds through miles
of snowy tundra in a movie, not big huge northern dogs licking

my kneecaps like I'm a steak dinner, their lips sneering back to reveal sharp yellowing teeth.

Canines.

A mosquito lands on my arm and I slap it down in time to see a blob of my own blood spilling free. In my pocket, my phone is as still as death. I want it to vibrate. I want, at least, for Daff to text me so I can feel like I'm still at home, still connected to somebody, somewhere, somehow, even if only through a bunch of texts that I'll never answer. I clench the phone in my hand, just to feel it, solid and familiar in my pocket, while I look frantically around the open space for a place to go that isn't here.

The dogs are snuffling and hot-breathed, pushing too hard against my legs. There seem to be too many of them all at once, and without thinking, I drop to the floor, rolled up in a ball. I think I say something.

I think what I say is *no.*

But the thing with these dogs is that they don't let up. A head pressed to my chest, another one in my face, licking licking and in the background, Dad laughing and laughing, like the funniest thing he's ever seen is his own kid, drenched in panic-sweat, under a thousand pounds of dog, on his plywood cabin floor.

11

I SLEEP BETWEEN SPIDER-MAN SHEETS IN A LOFT THAT
I get to by stairs that are so steep they are almost a ladder, a fact
that doesn't stop the dogs from following me up and filling the
available space with their breathing. It's a place that Dad had
clearly been using for storage, and to "get it ready," he simply shoved
the cases of cereal and wine and beer and soup to one side to make
room for a bed for me.

I dream of something dusty and wake up sneezing. "Cleaning"
is obviously a low priority for Dad, along with "home decoration"
and "hygiene," which makes him the opposite of Mom in yet
another way. She would have a heart attack if she saw this place.
She'd be bleaching the dogs, whose hair drifts around on surfaces
like it's hoping to eventually weave itself into a new dog. The
dogs themselves are sprawled widely, like men who spread their
legs open on subway seats. They sleep heaped up on the floor. And
when they are up, pacing around, they are too big for the space,
their claws clattering on the scratched hardwood, their breathing

taking up all the air. I hiss at them between my teeth and one looks at me and thumps his tail on the floor. *We aren't friends*, I tell him with my eyes, and he sighs like he gets it.

"They're friendly," Dad says. "They're the best dogs. You're going to love them. Man, I wish I'd had dogs when I was younger. They teach you so much, you know, about how to be human. They were sled dogs. It's a terrible story, how the owner rounded his dogs up and shot them when his business failed. Someone managed to save a few and I took these three. They are so so so great. They are the best. You've got to love them."

I nod and shrug. The nod-and-shrug being my primary way of communicating with Dad.

Their eyes glisten pale blue like a sky with the richness frozen out of it. They follow me around the main area of the cabin, which is kitchen/living room/dining room/every room. Dad's bedroom is stuck on the back, like an afterthought. There's no bathroom.

Like he's reading my mind, Dad goes, "Oh, yeah, I don't know why you didn't ask yesterday, ha ha, but there's no bathroom, it's an outhouse down the trail. Or, you know, pee behind a tree or whatever. Like I guess you did. Unless I should worry about kidney failure! No biggie. There's no one around."

I stare at him. Okay, sure. Fine. An outhouse down the trail. Why not? I think of our bathroom at home, the way Mom cleans between the tiles with a toothbrush soaked in Tilex. The way the water drips rustily into the drain, leaving a sad orange mark, like tears on the white face of a clown and how every day she's scrubbing at it with a Magic Eraser until every mark of it is eradicated again.

I whistle between my teeth and Dad jumps. The dogs don't shift.

"Yeah?" he says. "Did you say something?" His face is so hopeful. I hate him. There's a lump in my throat. I want to slam my hand in the door, or worse. I don't know what I want. I press my foot hard into the ground so my ankle predictably aches.

I snap my fingers and then the dogs come to me, giant heads nudging my legs, tails wagging. *Good dogs*, I say silently. *Good boys.* I don't know who I'm reminding. Me, or them. Maybe I just want to be the kind of guy who understands dogs in some profound way. Maybe I want to be a guy dogs like.

Why not?

Dad lies on the floor and they lick his face, paw his chest, rest on his legs.

I fight the urge to kick him. Getup, getup getup. You aren't five. He laughs like he doesn't care how stupid he looks. Grabs a dog and rubs its belly hard. The dog's eyes practically roll back in his head from joy. Man, those dogs love him.

I was five when Dad left. Mom has made a real effort to never say anything bad about him. She says things like, "He tries his best." And, "He just doesn't know." And, "We weren't right for each other." And, "He was never right for New York and it wasn't right for him." I try to imagine what really happened between them. Did he cheat? Lie? Drink? Hit her?

Did she hit him?

It's not like I'm going to ask.

I don't remember much about it. But I do remember how

Mom's voice would curl sharply up into the air like cut glass when she was angry. I remember how his edges seemed dulled and floppy in comparison. The way he'd slink out of the apartment, hunched and folded, and not come back for hours or days.

How my heart would race and stutter. He was like the opposite of a hero. He was soft in every wrong way. How much I hated him.

He gets up off the floor, pours cereal, slops milk in that spills over the side of the bowl. Takes a bite, crunching loudly. I make for the door. With a full mouth, Dad yells, *"Stop."* He runs into the kitchen and grabs a roll of paper towel, tears one off, and starts drawing frantically, like my life depends on it. The dogs thud down around me, like they know this will take forever so they may as well nap. I tap the screen of my phone, even though there are only two bars of signal and nothing is coming through.

"Signal here is kinda spotty," says Dad. "It's better down the beach a bit."

I type, *Tell Daisy, wazzzuuuuuuuuuuppppp.*

Send.

I close my eyes, feeling my message being carried into the cold marble box where The King's remains are probably liquefying.

I swallow hard.

Gag. Cough.

Recover.

I am okay, I tell myself. I am fine.

Daisy was The King's toy poodle. He carried her around in a purse for a few months. "It's a murse," he'd say, offended. "Not a freaking purse."

"Yeah," I'd say. "That's really manly, dude. A poodle in a purse."

He'd raise his fist as if he was about to belt me, then he'd laugh. *"Murse,"* he'd say.

We taught Daisy to play dead when someone said wazzup. We taught her to sit by saying roll over. We thought it was funny. It was probably pretty stupid, now that I think of it. A lot of things are a lot funnier at the time than when you look back on them, I guess.

Then one day he stopped bringing Daisy everywhere. "She's at home," he said. "She has diarrhea."

Turns out his dad kicked her so hard he punctured her liver with her own rib bone and she had to be put down.

Dad finishes his sketch and presents it with a flourish. It's a map to the best beach, which is dumb because I can see the beach out the window. This is an island. It is basically *all* beach. Anyway, mostly I really need to use the outhouse.

The cabin is perched on a point, the pebbly bay on one side and a sweep of sandstone beach carved by wind and water down the other. There is ocean all around. Behind us, back up in the forest, is the skeleton of the hotel that—according to Dad—will likely never be completed. He mumbles something about legal issues and cost of electricity and transportation. I've got to be honest, I'm not really listening.

There are no other cabins this far down the island. There are about a dozen of them about a mile up the coast. Dad says the people from there don't come down our end very often. He gets power from solar panels and Internet from the more populated island across the narrow pass where the tide runs so hard it makes whirlpools that I can see from here, through the not-too-clean glass of the sliding door to the deck.

I scrunch up his map and shove it into the back pocket of my shorts, like I'll ever look at it again.

"Watch for cougars," he says. "Not kidding. Haven't seen any this year, but they're probably around. The dogs can get aggressive, so I kinda worry. Don't get one of my dogs killed, you know what I mean? Not that they would. Or you would. Or—" He sighs. "Anyway, I have work to do. And you're practically grown up! Not that a cougar cares. You know what to do, right? If you see a cougar?"

I blink. I don't have a clue, but I'm not going to tell him that. For one thing, that would involve talking. He grins. "Right," he says. "No cougars in Brooklyn. At least, not feline ones. Ha ha. So . . . be big. Wave your arms. Big and loud. Not that the big cats want to eat you. Not really. They're scared of people. Besides, they'd rather eat a deer, I'm sure."

I nod once, fast. Big, loud, got it.

Like even a cougar would make me talk.

Not.

Dad's wrong about cougars in New York. There is one. Or was one. Daff and I went on this field trip to the Bronx Zoo last term for Science/Life class. I don't know where The King was. He was probably away: the Bahamas, Europe, or maybe only the Hamptons, where he liked to lie by the pool and read the classics. He said it was better than school, a more intelligent use of time. And he was probably right: the zoo was terrible to the point of being the most depressing place in the world. All these concrete enclosures and sad animals looking around and thinking, WTF? *This* is not my beautiful life.

I wondered if they dreamed of savannas where they had never

been, if sometimes they woke with a start to the sound of a snake slithering through their imaginary territory. If they thought about the kills they'd never make, the places where they'd never run.

It broke my heart, if I'm being honest.

There was a cougar in one of the concrete enclosures, stretched out in the sun like an overgrown house cat. Snoring.

"OMG, he's so cute!" Daff had said. She'd pressed her face up to the bars. "I am the Cougar Whisperer," she whispered. "Come to me, cougar."

The cat woke up. He sniffed the air.

"You won't think he's cute when he claws your face off," I'd said, pulling her back.

"Silly," she'd said. "Like they'd put a *face-clawing* cougar in the zoo."

"*Daff,*" I'd said. "Seriously? You think that this is a special cougar? One who has signed something saying, 'I will never claw off someone's face'? For real?"

"No!" She'd laughed. "He wouldn't. I can tell. He has soulful eyes. He has a gentle spirit."

She put her face back close, whispering like a crazy person. "Kitty, kitty, over there, come and lick my looooooovely hair."

I remember how he crouched low, staring at her. I remember how quickly he moved. I pulled her away so fast that she staggered a couple of times before finally she fell hard on her knees. She was so pissed. She'd been wearing shorts and her knees were skinned on the pavement, the skin cracked, her red flesh shining through.

"He couldn't have *reached* me," she'd snapped. "He was too far. He was caged. Idiot. Now I need Band-Aids."

And she was right. He couldn't have. There were two fences. There was no way.

"Is that how you thank me for saving your face?" I'd said, mock-heroically. "What happened to, 'You're my heeeeee-ro'?"

She'd smacked me on the arm and taken off running, blood bubbling through the wounds, streaking down her shins.

Of course she was only pretending to be mad. It never lasted.

". . . okay?" Dad said.

I blinked. Nodded. Yeah, dude, I thought. I'm just fine.

18

Dear Daff,

   This is an island.

   This is not an island like, say, Coney Island or like any
other island I have seen. The forest is crazy thick and deep
and unbelievably green and I can't even really describe it,
it's like the long exhalation of everything natural in the
world, like it's been sucked out of everywhere else and
dropped here. Every city and every crummy town and every
strip mall dreams of being a place like this. No kidding. I
can see the lights of Vancouver and the smog that hangs
over that city during the day, but it's too far away to hear it.
It's quiet here. And there are no lights, except the solar
lights we use after dark in the cabin. No streetlights or
shop lights or car headlights or anything. The darkness is
absolute. I feel like even my blood runs blacker somehow.
You know?

   There is nothing here.

No one.

I don't think I've ever been anywhere before where there aren't people and sounds, honking and cars and music and shouting and doors slamming and things crashing and so this is like suspended animation. It's like what I would imagine being in a coma is like or maybe like being dead.

Is it okay to say that?

No, probably not.

Too soon.

It will be too soon forever.

Things that will never be funny again:

1. All the stuff we used to do together.

2. Death.

Anyway, skip over that. Pretend I didn't say that. Hey, I could just hit Delete. And maybe I will.

I could start over like this:

Dear Daff,

The trees are so old, they make you catch your breath. You can feel them growing. You know they are bored because you and your problems are so tiny and they've been here forever already, pulling in the carbon dioxide from generations of lungs, for hundreds of years. They've already seen everything there is to see and there is nothing new about you. Some are so big that you could stand ten people around them in a circle, holding hands, and they wouldn't be able to reach all the way around. They go up to the clouds like steeples and the clouds seem to stick and hang on them, like they are thinking about settling in for a landing.

I've got to be honest, they make me think about God. Or the gods. Or whatever. No? Maybe? Yes?

Probably no.

It is so quiet that I can hear myself breathing. Remember that thing we read about how they put people in a completely sound-free room and most people were clawing to get out within minutes?

Those people would hate it here. They would be splashing out into the sea, swimming for the safety of the city.

It also feels like a place where a cougar might surprise you with a mitt-sized paw to the jugular. The dogs stopped all at once, growling, while I was walking just now. Then they started barking into the shrubbery that grows along the trail. True fact: I was scared to death. But it's not like the cougar would have stood a chance against these guys. Dad has given them awful names: Willy and Sunny and Buddy. Seriously. Don't tell my dad, but I've renamed them: Maximus and Apollo and Zeus. Gods of the Forest. Well, really of the snow, but they seem to like it here fine. Somehow when they aren't inside the cabin, I'm not afraid of them, not even a bit. They fill up this space the way they should.

But you don't like dogs that are too big for purses, right? You know, I just remembered that Daisy was a gift from you. Why did you give Daisy to him? You had to know his dad *would hate her. I remember asking you and I remember you said, "It's a special occasion, right?" And he said, "Yeah, it is." And you said, "Tell him." And he wouldn't tell. I guess I know that you hooked up with him. I guess that's what it was about. And I'm as stupidly jealous now as I was then, even though I know there was nothing after. Maybe. Or was there? I don't know, Daff. You always left your hand on his arm a little too long after trying to get his attention. Yeah, I'm sure you're hitting Delete now. I would, too. I don't know why and I don't know why and I don't know why this is how I feel, but I do. I feel like you're my person, Daff. That's what I feel. But now you aren't, because you can't be, because it killed him.*

Maybe.

If it wasn't an accident, I mean.

If.

If.

If.

What if it wasn't an accident, Daff?

I think it wasn't.

I think it was.

Eff this. I'm hitting Delete.

I'm not hitting Delete.

I don't know what the right thing is to do anymore. I am so lost, Daff. These trees are so tall, reaching up higher than anything and I could climb one to the top. And then what? It would be an accident or it wouldn't.

I don't want to talk about The King.

I can't write to you (even without sending it, which I won't) without him being right here, beside me, giving me that look that's half laughing with me and half laughing at me and I can't do this. I can't do anything. I'm not in Brooklyn eating a bag of frozen shrimp from downstairs on the front stoop, waiting for you and The King to come and get me, waiting for something to start.

I'm here, I'm nowhere. It's like being someplace that doesn't exist, which is good, because then I don't have to exist either. I don't have to be Sharkboy, the kid whose kinda-famous best friend died when he fell off a building owned by his über famous dad. I can just be. No one even has to know my name.

Not that there is anyone here to ask.

You know, I don't even know what this island is called. I only know that it's an island. One with towering fir trees, crashing surf, and a couple hundred pounds of dog tearing around me in the six-foot-high salal, flushing out a deer who ricochets away over fallen trees and vanishes up a fern-drenched bluff, performing the best freaking parkour I've ever seen.

Forests are messy. I never realized how messy until now.

Kind of like life. You think it's going to be one way, all clearly drawn, and then you get close to it. And it's just a pile of dead branches, leaves still falling down on you, bark that's been half eaten away by rot and animals. Dirt. Tree roots in inconvenient places, bulging like some kind of terrible "condition" through the ground.

If this could be more surreal, I'm not sure how.
I'll talk to you soon. Catch ya on the flip side.
Peace out.
I miss you. I hate you. I love you. I blame you. Etc.
Love,
JC

19

I WALK IN THE WOODS A LOT.

My phone makes a warm square on my leg through the thin material of my shorts, heating up while it searches for enough signal to not send the stuff in my drafts folder that I'll never send. The unsendable. The marine air tints everything with a cool chill that takes the heat out of the afternoon. The forest path is narrow and underused. I have to watch my feet so I don't trip on roots or fallen branches. Once, I step off the path altogether to go around a rotting tree and figure out pretty quickly what stinging nettle looks like. My legs burn and the skin tightens and itches all at once. The trail winds along the shoreline. Sandstone beaches pocked with tide pools on my right. Forests dark and heavy on my left, interspersed with sunny meadows that are either mossy or grassy, the grass itself having turned yellow. It's the kind of pretty that makes you take photos and wish you had someone to send them to. The light is freaking golden. Mom would go crazy for this light. She has a thing about light. *Look at it,* she'd say. *Just look at it.* I don't know how many times I've found myself in the kitchen, staring at the way the sunlight pools on the floor and makes a tiny rainbow because of the bevel in the glass, rolling my eyes at her, shrugging, whatever.

I miss Mom. I'd never say that. But.

I pull my phone out of my pocket and take a picture. I send it to her.

Dear Son, What pretty light! she texts back right away. *Gorgeous light. I love. Am in Amsterdam. It was rainy today. Now it's moony. Our hero stepped out with a waitress from the restaurant. Aren't twenty-five choices enough? These people! Crazy town. xooox Missing you.*

Mom has always treated text messaging like it's a letter. She doesn't really quite get how it's just a conversation. It doesn't have to work that way, with an opening and closing. But that's how she is.

OK, I type back. *Bye Mom.*

I walk and walk and try not to think of anything, which means I think of everything, which means by the time the path pops out in a sheltered bay—the "good beach," I guess—I'm tired from thinking too much.

Pink mist. Chewed gum all over the concrete. Cigarette butts and puke. The near-silent *click* of journalists' cameras. Daff's dress. Her lips. Daff, Daff, Daff.

I look at my sneakered feet on the hard-packed dirt path. I have blisters. Stupid shoes are too small. A butterfly flies by in a crooked flight path as if to say, *Seriously, man, get over yourself.* There are a lot of different birds calling. The waves gently push in and out on the beach. In the far distance, a boat's engine choppily echoes across the sea. The smell of the sea makes me feel like nothing matters, at the same time reminding me that everything does, and it's so much. It's too much. I just want it all to stop.

And then I'm crying again. Awesome.

I sit.

I stop.

I guess I don't move for a long time.

My phone buzzes. Daff. *Je peux parler le francaise aussi, jrk-face. Appelez-moi, svp.*

Jrkface n'est pas en français, I reply. I hesitate before hitting Send. Too funny? Too friendly? I think about her lips. I think about how she said, "He died for love. It was, like, poetry. But bad poetry. The kind that breaks your heart for the wrong reason." I think about her red dress. I press Delete instead.

Je regrette tout, I want to say, but don't.

Eventually, the tide rolls out and a sandbar rises up like a huge circular island that stretches beyond the driftwood-lined shore. The air is the perfect temperature. It's a perfect day. A few dinghies are tied to long lines, resting on their hulls on the driftwood like beached whales. The mooring buoys bobbing in the calm water are all empty, the handful of cabins that stare down into the bay stare vacantly at the water, nobody there.

I go down to the warm stone island that rises in the center of the bay like a spine. The rock is warm. A bird squawks loud and low and nearby, skimming the surface of the still, green water. I sit and take my shoes off and squish my blisters, which hurts and feels right.

I went to the Hamptons with The King once and he dared me to dive into the curling surf, which I did. Well, obviously. The waves pushed me down so hard that my belly was scraped raw on the sand below. Then I did it again. And again. By the end of that week, I was a pro, diving through the waves like a freaking dolphin while The King sat on the shore and shouted about rip currents, like a girl.

He never swam. He said black people weren't made to go in the water. He said, "Watch the Olympics, man. It's a white dude's sport. We have heavier bones." I tried to drag him in and he panicked, pushed me hard, ran from me, staggering in the sand to get away.

I didn't try again. You had to know with him how far he was willing to go. He'd do anything crazy that was high up or otherwise stupid—bungee jump off a crane in a parking lot; rappel down the side of one of his dad's stupid buildings for charity; tightrope walk anywhere, anytime—but he wouldn't ever ever ever swim.

You have to respect that about a person once you know what their fear is. Once you know why they are afraid.

The sea here is different from in the east, that's for sure. There is no surf, only a few ripples rolling in and out of a line of mucky shoreline detritus, seaweed and wood chips and a couple of plastic bottles and dead crabs. Out beyond the empty mooring buoys that speckle the water, there's a raft with a lone deck chair angled to the sun. After a lifetime in Brooklyn, the abandoned feel of this place is both a huge relief and also terrifying in a horror-movie-setting kind of way. I mean, really, sincerely, no one *would* hear you scream.

It's too quiet.

Too pretty.

Too nature-y.

Too much like something that is nothing to do with me.

A seagull squawks and I jump about a mile. One of the dogs barks at me, staring at me like I have something to give him.

Nothing, I tell him in my head. He seems to get that. "Nothing," I try out loud. Because why not? No one is listening and there aren't rules to this. But then my throat spasms painfully and I start to cough. Choking. I'm choking. It takes me a minute to catch my breath, to swallow smoothly. To breathe.

It's the first word I've spoken in months. "NOTHING," I yell, because I *can*. My voice is loud and unfamiliar and bounces off the glassy surface of the water, ricocheting around the bay.

I'm starting to see why people went crazy in that quiet room. The dead silence that follows is worse than before. More dead. Deader. The deadest? What's worse than dead?

Dead is following me around like the dogs, now flopped out in the shade on wet sand. The heavy wet breath of *dead* won't leave me alone. I strip off my T-shirt and wrap my phone up in it and rest it on the rock, then pick my way over the lumpy, painful pebbles to where the sand smooths out. It sinks under my feet, occasionally squirting water at me through the round holes made by clams. The water is colder than I expected, and up close it isn't as clear as I would have thought. Even beyond the tide line, wood chips and seaweed and jellyfish clutter up the surface. The corpse of a crab. It smells of salt and decay. Weeds growing up from the bottom brush by my legs. I try to ignore them and what they might be hiding. I wade deeper. Beside me, a huge living jellyfish with a red center slides by on the current, gelatinous as a raw egg. I dive in anyway, the water closing over my head, my ears full of the rush of cold silence. I surface, spluttering, and then start to swim. My lips taste salty and strange. It's different from swimming at the Y, weirder, the water is thicker and lighter and I'm buoyed up by it.

I swim past the end of the bay, then farther still. It feels like I'm breaking some kind of rule, like someone is going to start shouting at me to stop. To go back. It feels dangerous and also like being free. I could swim forever. I could swim to Vancouver. I mean, I'd drown first, but I could try.

I could drown. What would Daff say at my funeral?

Instead, I keep stroking until I get to a sandstone reef that rises like its own private island about a hundred feet from shore. A group of fat seals notice me and then slide, one by one, resentfully, into the sea, bobbing a few feet away. Staring. Pulling myself up onto the rock is harder than you'd think, it's nothing like the side of a pool, all clean lines and straight edges. It's slippery and sharp and uneven. I cut my foot on a barnacle. The blood beads up like it's nothing to do with me. Not my blood. I walk up onto the crest of the stone, leaving a trail of red marks on the bright green seaweed that carpets the sandstone like fur on a seal's back. Tiny hermit crabs stab my bare feet. I sweep some away and sit down. The sandstone is pocked with holes that are full of water, finger-sized. It's hard not to stick your fingers into them. The water cupped inside them is hot from the sun.

From here, I can see even more cabins nestled in the woods that at first you wouldn't know were there, camouflaged by the trees as they are. One of them is beautiful, it looks like someone's dream home. The next one is half-built, building materials rotting in piles leaning up against a falling frame. The next is painted the same green-brown of the trees, like its owner was hiding it on purpose.

Everything is still, like it's holding its collective breath.

I sit on the reef, my feet in a warm pool of salt water, which smells terrible. There are huge piles of bird crap and who-knows-what-else everywhere. Time passes and the water starts rising and the island that I'm on starts shrinking. Tide. The skin on my back feels tight and burned by an afternoon in the sun. I look into the green water, at the brown seaweed waving there, and I close my eyes and dive back in, twisting and turning exactly like the seals had, getting only a bit tangled in that kelp, which is slippery and strong in my grasp.

The water is too cold here for most species of shark, but I know there are mud sharks down there, somewhere underneath me. Dogfish. I try to think what else would be here, in these waters. Maybe threshers. Six gills and seven gills. Angel sharks. Blue sharks, which are everywhere.

Mako. Hammerheads. Great Whites. It's really unlikely—they like the open ocean better—but it's *possible*.

I plunge down as deep as I can and open my eyes. A forest of kelp stems moves gently back and forth. A rusty gas can is stuck between two rocks. Even here, away from everything, we dump our crap into the water. It's pathetic, that's what it is. We act like the ocean doesn't matter, when really, it's the only thing that does. I stay down for as long as I can, until my eyes feel like they are going to bulge out of my head and I have to breathe.

Sometimes, you have to come up for air.

20

I HAVE TO SWIM HARD AGAINST THE CURRENT TO GET back to the bay where I left my clothes. The tide has completely covered the sand with knee-deep icy water from the strait. At first, I think I've swum back to the wrong place, but then I see the dogs lolling and panting right where I left them, the water lapping ever closer to their resting spot. I'm shivering, my hands and feet blue-tinged. I need to lie on the rock for a while and warm up. It's not until I'm awkwardly pulling myself up on the shrinking rock that I realize I am not alone.

Sitting next to my shirt, her back to me, is a girl. She has earbuds in and she is bent over a book. The sun glances off her bare shoulders, which are already coppery brown.

I clear my throat, but she doesn't move at first. I take another step and she turns around. Stares.

"Boo," she says. She grins wide, showing a mouthful of white teeth, held in place by a thin silvery line of braces. Her white-blond hair doesn't go with her brown skin. She looks like a negative, a reverse of a normal person. Her face is sprayed with dark freckles. She pulls out one earbud and wrinkles her nose. "Your stuff is in my spot. But I guess I'll forgive you." She shrugs. "I moved your shirt. I'm glad I didn't drop your phone. How was I supposed to know it was in there, anyway? Tide's coming up, so it doesn't matter where you sit. We'll both lose our island in a while."

I know she's waiting for me to say something so I try, I really do, but no words come out, so I shrug while what comes out of my mouth sounds like growling. I cough.

"You okay?" she says. "Cat got your tongue? That's what my gran would have said. That's her place." She points up into the woods where I can see nothing but trees. "Ours now though," she adds. "She's dead. Gran, that is. She died. Yeah, Gran died. And anyway, she left it to us. So now it's mine and my mum's and my little brother's. My dad is . . . Anyway, my brother, Charlie, he's napping. He has to nap. He's super hyper and then he crashes. And Mum's at your—" She stops herself, tapping her lips like she physically is going to stop the words from coming out. "Ohhhhhhkay," she says. "Not gonna lie. My mum's got a thing with your dad, if you know what I mean. They are pretty into each other. It's cute, you know? If you can avoid looking at their tongues when they kiss. Seriously. So. Anyway. Yeah." She looks at me again, hard, like she can see through me. Her eyes are greenish, flecked with gold, or maybe that's only the reflection of the sinking sun. "I already know all about you and your dead friend and not talking and shark stuff so I'm not going to pretend that I don't know because that would

111

be . . . sort of a lie, I guess. Should I have said that? No, probably not, huh. Well, too bad. I'm just honest. I'm an honest person."

I sit, not because I want to talk to her, but because I need to get closer to the rock. I need some warmth. The stone feels like a hot relief under my skin. The thing with sandstone is that it looks smooth but it's really not. The surface is a bit rough, sandpapery. I rub my fingers on it a bit, just because. I wonder if I'm erasing my fingerprints. I kind of hate people who say they are honest, out loud, because it usually is an excuse for saying really rude things. "Just being honest!" they tag, right after they've said something about you that hurts.

"Sooooooo," she says. "Awkward, huh. Here we are, you and me, on this rock, on an island in the middle of nowhere and I have to do the talking because you don't, which is . . . well, it's a little weird, I gotta tell you. I'm Kelby, by the way. So hi. Helllooo in there. You are JC, otherwise known as Sharkboy, but that sounds kinda stupid, if you ask me, so I'm gonna go ahead and call you JC. Which, also, I don't know. Jesus Christ? My mum is super religious, so she's the one who noticed that actually, but I know, it's John Christopher or whatever, but those don't fit either. Hey, I could make up my own name for you! Like, I don't know, Snort." She laughs.

I like her laugh. It's just there, a full laugh, happy and open. Daff's laugh is a bit shrill, a bit trying-too-hard, a bit overly girly, but also perfect. So what do I know? Nothing. Jesus, not everything is about *Daff*. But man, she'd like calling me Snort. I kind of grin, kind of don't, pretend I'm looking out into the bay, into the new shadows on the green sea, languorously reaching for us across the rising water.

"So, Snort," she says. "What I'm going to do now is put my music back on again and go back to my book and if I think of something to say, I'll say it. And you can sit there and be all pensive and cute and whatnot and think deep things about sharks and death. Oh, crap." She pauses. "Okay, scratch that last part, Snort. I didn't say anything about you being cute. The fact of your cuteness does not mean that we will be friends. Technically," she adds, "you're not my type. Too . . . soft." She picks up her book and holds it up, like she's inspecting it for bugs. She shakes it out.

"Sometimes wasps crawl in between the pages," she continues. "Anyway, we can be friends. But only if you want. I like having boys as friends. I'm not so good with girls. Girls, in case you didn't know, are way complicated. Boys are simple. I like that. And you, Snort, being so quiet and all, seem particularly simple. Your simplicity is appealing. As a friend. Not as anything else. So stop looking at my boobs, okay? You're kinda weirding me out. Enough. Now I'm reading. I'm reading this book. It's not very good. It's about the end of the world, the apocalypse. Honestly, it's freaking me out a bit. Now I'm just going to stop talking and I'm gonna kind of pretend that it *is* the end of the world, only we don't know it, because we are here, and who knows what is going on in the world over there?" She waves her hand toward Vancouver, which is completely hidden by smog and haze. I nod. I understand that. Yeah, it could be the end of the world.

It has been the end of the world.

The end of my world.

I wonder if she'd get that, if I said it out loud. Which I won't. I mean, I'm not opening up to a stranger for no good reason. But I can't stop staring at her, not just because it's taking me a while to filter through everything she said, but because she is insanely cute. Which is kind of true of all girls though, that's the problem. If you look at them, separate from a crowd, alone, you can see all kinds of things about them that'll make your heart stop. The way their lips are. Eyelashes. The shape of their face. A guy could fall for any of these people. They are all amazing. When you look at them, without distractions, I mean. Without comparing them to Daff.

I don't know how anyone ever chooses. How anyone ever knows that this one girl is the only girl they want to be with forever. I get dizzy from all the pretty girls, if I'm being honest.

Settle down, Casanova, The King would say. *You don't need the drama. Girls are trouble, your basic nightmare. Sooner or later, they're saying nasty crap about you on Facebook, then you won't be so, ooooooh, look at those eyelashes.*

I can practically hear him saying it, that's how real it feels. I wave my hand through the air beside me, just in case.

Her eyelashes really are unbelievable though. They make a shadow on her cheek. It's the angle of the sun or a trick of the light.

I pick up my phone, which feels extra hot from sitting on the rock in the sun. It's hard to see the screen. I write, *You're not my type either.*

It's not like I can send it. It's not like I have her number. I hit Cancel. The pigeons do not swoop. Then, because my phone is in my hand, I type, *Weather's great, wish you were here,* then take a photo of Kelby, and hit Send, the *swoop* curling around something in my chest and pulling.

Text failed, it says. *Try again?*

No.

My heart is pounding extra hard. Text failed. Try again?

No.

No.

No.

The dogs wander up from the sand, panting, shoving their faces into my legs. They look hot and thirsty and annoyed. I take my eyes off the girl and try to stand, pushing the dogs away.

"I don't want you to feel weird," she says, without looking up. "Even though the not-talking thing is totes weird, obvi. But we're all weird. Everyone is. I mean, look at me. I look normal. I have a normal life and a normal boyfriend and everything. But I'm not normal either. I'm really not. Inside, I'm not. But maybe everyone feels like that, like everyone else is normal and inside, we're all like, Yeah, but not *me*. Stuff happens. But it doesn't change, say, your nose. Or the way your eyes are arranged on your face. But it changes *you*." She stops and starts scratching her fingernail into the sun-tanned brown of her leg, leaving a white-flaked heart.

The water is rising now with serious intent. Tide. I don't know if I've ever experienced tide before, at least not like this. Not like watching a bay fill up and empty. I don't want to interrupt but there's no clear way to get in to shore now without wading. The dogs jump down and swim for it, their fur spreading out around them like feathers in the water.

"We all get changed," she says. "That's all."

I cough, sounding like my mom. *Ribbit ribbit.*

"Okay," she says. "Our whole lives, things are going to happen to us. Sometimes because of us. Sometimes nothing to do with us.

But we can't stop these happenings. And we can't help being changed by them. I think of it like . . . seasons. Like the leaves on the trees. Hey, you want to know a great word? 'Abscission.' It's my favorite word. You know how leaves fall off the trees in the autumn? Well, the trees actually kind of throw them off. Did you know that? They eject the leaves! I think that's so awesome. But I guess what I mean is that the seasons happen, no matter what. Does that sound cheesy? Maybe it is. But yeah, change. We're all changing. It's like . . ." She pauses again. "Evolution, I guess. It's like we're evolving constantly. It's unstoppable." She lies back on the rock and I pretend to not look at how her breasts fall sideways a bit and I shouldn't be looking, but I am. "It's like because you aren't talking, I have to talk too much." She closes her eyes, like she's exhausted from the effort it takes to talk to me. Her book slides down the rock and I should rescue it but I don't. I want it to float away.

I feel dismissed by the way her eyes are shut, by the way she stopped talking. And I'm mad. I don't know why I am, but I am. I hope for mud sharks. Bull sharks would be better, chewing at my legs. But they wouldn't be up here. No way. Too cold. Tears sting my eyes. *Abscission*. Maybe The King's dad's building *abscised* him. Is that a word? Abscised? It's not that good a word, not to me.

It's hard to move fast in water, and buried partially in the soft sand sharp shells are poking through, slicing into my bare blistered feet. Once I get up onto the logs, I feel like I'm safer. Safe from her, safe from talking. My ankle rolls and crackles and throbs. The toilet was a long time ago, but still, it never healed right. It clicks back into place as I land heavily on a rock. I open my mouth and swear. Then, louder, I yell, *"Bye."*

She sits up. Waves. Stares.

"Hey," she shouts, her voice amplifying over the bay. "I thought you didn't talk!"

"I don't!" I yell over my shoulder, running now, jumping from log to log, my feet somehow knowing where to land, and I sprint hard up the sandstone slope into the woods, barely feeling the path under my bare feet, my shoes forgotten on the rocky shore, the dogs racing after me like it's their full-time job to stay near me, it's their duty to nip at my heels.

21

I JUST WANT TO STOP REMEMBERING, BUT NONE OF IT
will go away, like my brain is on a ride that it can't get off, which
makes me think of rides, which makes me think of that time we
climbed up the roller coaster track after the park was closed. Daff
was so tiny down there on the ground yelling, "Come down! Come
on. You're gonna kill yourselves!" But her laughter bubbled up and
urged us on. Truth: we'd both do anything to make her laugh her
crazy laugh like that. The King stood tall, bowed elaborately. Daff
got it on her phone for our parkour YouTube channel, the one that's
all over *Gawker* now, the ones of us showing off. She was doubled
over laughing, eventually, at whatever we were shouting, her laughter driving us higher and higher into the darkness. We were spider
monkeys, that's what it felt like, arms and legs swinging and searching and then finding holds. *Scampering*. We were so fast, you'd get
dizzy from watching, the track lit up by bulbs that you could see
the filaments in, yellow and flickering like tiny torches lighting up
a runway and we were the planes, soaring to touch down, I can't

explain how it was flying, how it *was* freedom, even though we could have fallen, almost fell, but didn't fall.

And at the top of the highest loop, I looked down and was hit by a wave of vertigo so intense that my stomach threatened to heave itself out of me, my eyes lost anything to hold on to, and I couldn't tell which way was up. Sometimes when you're diving, you lose the surface, your inner ear messes up and then *bam*, up is down, down is up, everything is tilted. Well, I lost the surface for a second, the stars and the bulbs got mixed up and I felt like I was going to fall up and out into space and be gone forever, I had to drop to my knees and hold on.

I *would* have fallen if The King hadn't been there, right behind me.

Or maybe I would have jumped, I don't know. Because that possibility is always there, like a frame around a picture. *What if I jumped.*

Not because I wanted to die but because sometimes you get that feeling, that one split second when you almost let go because you believe you *could* actually fly, for real, like you could almost force your arms to become wings, like there are feathers there that no one can see. Feathers waiting to help you fly. You can practically feel your arms and legs scrabbling in the air, failing (or flying, soaring) and the ground so far away but at the same time so close and the confusion inside you when that happens and that's vertigo, that's what it feels like. I teetered. I know I did. I thought about feathers. You don't ever want to think about feathers.

I wonder if The King thought about feathers.

I didn't fall. The King grabbed the back of my shirt, the collar cut into my neck and my breath had nowhere to go. Strangling, my hands flew up to my throat and he shoved me down hard onto the track, my hands slipping between the ties, skin peeling back like I was a ripe piece of fruit, blood seeping from the soft pastel place inside my wrists. "Oh man," I said. "That's gonna leave a mark." He laughed, his hand resting on my head, like he was giving me benediction.

Son, you are *saved*.

Amen, amen to that.

I came down slow, so slow, too slow. I wobbled down on shaking legs, hands dripping blood, pretending to be laughing, trying not to puke. He came down the same way he went up: full tilt, running, jumping, a handstand on the crest of the upside-down curve, flipping where he shouldn't have flipped but making it anyway. I took a shortcut down the struts, hand over hand, foot over foot, climbing down them like a ladder with too much space between each step.

"Thanks," I said, when I was finally steady, pavement underfoot. "Don't know what happened."

"I wouldn't let you fall, man," he said. "I love you." He reached out his hand and cupped my chin and . . .

Or no.

I don't know what I'm

There was a minute when I thought he was going to

I would never

Adrenaline was surging through both of us. An owl swooped down behind him from the darkness, so silently we both screamed.

It dropped a dead mouse, which landed near The King's feet. He flinched backward, kicking at it. Stepped back and fell over on the hard concrete ground.

"Well," he drawled. "*That* was stupid. Your turn to save me, I guess. Makes us even."

I think it was raining, which must be wrong because I also remember stars. The memory is blurry and I can't quite get hold of all of it. I think I reached out my hand and pulled him up. I think I laughed. I think he laughed. I think we were laughing right there in the shadow of that coaster that didn't kill us with all those stars up there flickering like an audience. But maybe not. *Memory* is a word that slithers away suddenly, darting faster than it should be able to move at all.

I do remember that he lay back flat, stretched out, hands crossed over his chest. He closed his eyes. Smiled like someone in a coffin, pinched and fake. I remember that he hugged me hard, arms around my back. He tipped his head back and screamed up at the sky, animal-loud and raw.

He was so powerful, more powerful than anyone I'd ever met or known. He had this

I don't know

He was

Then Daff was saying, "I gotta pee, I gotta pee," and The King grabbed her and kissed her hard on her cheek, bit her really, and she doubled over, peed her pants, and we were laughing and couldn't stop, not ever, and the laughter was the same as falling through space, leaving a huge distance between where we were on the ground and where we'd been, up there at the top, nothing above us but those stars and the crescent thumbnail of the lightly veiled moon.

I stop running, out of breath. I might be crying, I can't tell, but I know for sure that I feel like puking, the stitch in my side is pulling me up so tight that stretching makes me feel like I'll snap myself in two. I bend over, hand on a rotten stump, focus on the yellow grass, green moss, gray rock. I lift my eyes and stare across the strait, rising now with white caps, the wind blowing at me seems to have come from out of the blue, the angry sea is whipping its fury into my face. I pull my phone out of my pocket to take a photo— the buildings on the Vancouver skyline are illuminated by the sinking sun behind me and look like they are on fire, a scene that was basically made for Instagram—but then I stop. It's too beautiful and it's not what I mean to say. If a picture is worth a thousand words then each one of these is the wrong word. I angle the phone up toward the ancient trees and take a picture and send it to my mom. She'll know what I mean, even if I'm not exactly clear myself.

22

I CAN HEAR THEIR VOICES AS I GET CLOSER TO THE
cabin. Dad. A woman. A kid. Someone laughs. A glass clatters to
the deck. A boy yells, "I DIDN'T DO IT!" Someone shushes him,
laughing. Music plays tinnily on a crappy stereo. I don't want to get
closer to this private party but I'm starving, so unless I want to eat
something I've picked out of the woods, I have to go past them to
get to the kitchen.

They go quiet when they see me. Then Dad breaks the silence.
"Hey!" he says. "Did you swim? Did you meet Kelby? She went
down to say hi. This is my . . ." His voice fades. "Anyway, this is
Charlie, and he's great. Oh, and his mom, Darcy." On the *Darcy*,
his voice cracks, giving him away.

She's pretty like a woman in a shampoo commercial for some
kind of organic brand.

Too pretty for my dad.

Darcy looks nervous, her smile is crookedly questioning. She's
freckly and overly tanned like her daughter but her hair is long and

blown back by the wind. She smiles like an aging supermodel. I force myself to smile back. Raise my fingers in a sort of salute, sort of wave.

"Hiiiiiii," she says, drawing it out long enough for me to know she's uncomfortable. "Good to meet you." Her hand goes up to her throat where it finds a cross on a chain that she twists while she smiles. "I've been looking forward to meeting you. Hi," she repeats.

Dad's hand is resting on Charlie's arm in a way that it never casually rested on mine, but the kid swats his arm away. Hard. Dad flinches.

"Oh, hello to you, too, scruffy beasts," Darcy says, holding out her hand. Then, "My favorite pups." The dogs break away from me and rub their faces on her like she's made out of steak. Burger, I think. *Burger.*

The King used to rank girls as Burgers or Fries. The Burgers were the ones with something to them, like Daff. The Fries were fun but meaningless, empty calories. He usually hooked up with Fries. Well, always. The girls from school who would relentlessly text him after he hooked up with them. The girls from other places who would appear, suddenly, in front of him on the sidewalk, smiling awkwardly, pretending not to be upset, playfully punching him on the arm, and saying, "Hey, you said you'd call." Sometimes he got their names wrong on purpose, or he'd squint at them, hesitating before getting it right, like he really had to think. He said it made them like him more and who knows, maybe they did. He didn't like them, though. I could never figure that out, why he kept it up, kept flirting, kept smiling, kept holding on to them after the party ended.

"Slut," I'd call him, and he'd say, "Listen, you're clearly jealous. I should give you lessons." And I'd say, "No thanks, I'm saving myself for—" and he'd say, "College?" And I'd say, "Nah, for someone who'd have me." But I meant, *For Daff.*

Darcy clears her throat and says, "So hey, join us! We're just talking and . . . you know, there's a meteor shower for the next few nights, so we're waiting. Want a burger?"

"I can throw one on the grill, son," says Dad, in his too-jovial voice.

I shoot him a withering glance.

"We also have tofu!" she says, rubbing Zeus vigorously behind the ears. "Right, Sunny? *Mmmmm,* tofu. This one loves it," she adds.

The dogs look at me as if to say, *We love her! Why don't you love her! Love her already! Love! Love! Love!*

I glare at them. They are love vacuums, the three of them, sucking it all up like it matters more than food or water, more than anything. What do they know? I shake my head slowly. No.

Darcy says, "Hey, did you notice how Sunny has one brown eye and one blue eye? Legend has it that means he can see heaven and earth at the same time."

I stare. Is it possible for anyone to go five minutes around here without mentioning heaven? Without making me choke on *death*?

Seriously.

Of course I noticed his eyes.

The kid runs over to where I'm standing, plants himself in

front of me. His hair is dirty. Actually, his whole self is dirty, but in that way that makes him seem cleaner, somehow. Wholesome. Like he's a part of this island and not part of the real world. The sinking sun makes his hair shine like pure gold.

My stomach growls.

"How come you don't talk?" he says. "They told me not to ask you."

I nod. *That's right, kid. Don't ask.*

"Are you sort of like . . . an idiot?" he whispers. "Like sort of slow?"

I nod again. Yes, I am sort of *an idiot*. A slow idiot. Slow to understand. Slow to catch up. Slow to figure anything out. The words clatter like rusty nails in my brain, too sharp. Dangerous.

"Fucking idiots," The King's dad shouted that day he picked us up from the police station where we'd been taken in for jumping on cars in a parking complex, for setting off alarms. *"Why can't you be fucking normal? Why can't you play hockey like goddamn normal kids? Or goddamn basketball, you jerkwads."*

"I'm too short," The King said, "though Mr. JC Sharkboy here, he can slay a team single-handedly, slam-dunk all those shots, *plip plop*, like it's his full-time gig, yo." I said, "I don't play, actually." His dad prickled with rage, tiny white sprays of light around him like something otherworldly. Alive. His jaw clenched, his muscles there as overdeveloped as an athlete's pecs.

"Must get boring," the boy singsongs. "Being, you know," he whispers, *"mute.* Wanna go fishing?" He has an ice-cream bucket in his hand and he waves it at me. I raise an eyebrow. "For minnows," he says. "In the tide pools, duh. Tide's coming in, not much more time."

I shake my head no, and walk by him, up the last two steps, past Dad and Darcy.

"Is he okay? I hope Charlie didn't upset him. Poor kid," I hear her say. "Did I step in it with that thing about heaven? I didn't think—"

I slam the door on Dad's awkward laugh. It's okay to be rude here in the middle of nowhere, when you are so empty inside it's like your stomach is grabbing for your ribs, desperate to devour something, anything to fill it up. I make a sandwich and then go upstairs to eat it. It's hot. Every bit of the warmth of the day seems trapped in the stifling space. The air wants to curl away from my lungs. I open the window as wide as I can, letting in a clump of fir needles and a mosquito that aims for my ear immediately. I swat at it. The sea air drifts in, like it can hardly bother. I can see the kid crouched down on the shoreline, scooping his bucket through a tide pool. He looks up and waves. I raise my hand in what is quickly becoming my signature move. The goodbye salute.

I lie down on the rumpled sheets and crack a beer that I've swiped from Dad's stash. It's warm and tastes like parties and things I've regretted doing, but I drink it anyway. I fire up the laptop. I can't access the Internet—the connection seems to come and go here—but I don't care. It's not like I wanted to stare at Daff's pictures and love her and hate her and feel more than I can feel right now. It's not like I was going to answer the fifteen e-mails that she's sent since the funeral. It's not like I was going to go to The King's memorial page and hate everyone who wrote anything there. *We'll miss you, bro! Catch ya on the flip side!* It's not like I was going to Google the story again and read about it again and relive it again and be mad again and be sad again and everything keeps happening again and again and again. Maybe that's what life is: lather, rinse, repeat. Emphasis on the *repeat*.

I stare at the "connection unavailable" screen for a while, then I start watching *Sharkwater*, which I've mostly memorized. I fall asleep dreaming of the blood in the water, which congeals into the jellyfish I saw in the bay, red-bellied and ominous, which is lifted onto the flat palm of the girl with the white hair, Kelby, who spins around and morphs into Daff, laughing and twirling away on feathery wings up into the darkening blue of the summer sky.

If only my dreams were obvious or something, right?

For the first time since April, I don't dream of The King. I don't see his face as he flips backward into the volcano that swallows him as effortlessly as plankton disappearing into the baleen of a passing whale. I don't dream of him at all.

23

WHEN I WAKE UP, MY MOUTH IS THICK AND DRY AND
sticky. It's fully dark but the voices are still chattering on the deck.
The air is dense with the smell of burned burgers and fire-pit
smoke. The boy is curled up on the couch, asleep with the dogs,
breathing in god-knows-what-kind-of terrible old couch mold. Dad
and Darcy are sitting on a bench a short way down the point, heads
bent together. From here, they could be anyone. They could be teen-
agers. They could be me and Daff but the hair is wrong, as is the
way they are sitting. Everything is wrong. I shudder. There is a huge
moon hanging over the strait that looks like a prop from a stupid
Broadway musical. I half expect them to burst into a song-and-dance
number, tap dancing along the sandstone bluff.

The girl with the white hair is playing solitaire on the driftwood table. *Kelby*.

"Hey," she says. "Again. Hey again. You. Look, I'm sorry. This
is going to be weird if you hate me. Please don't hate me."

I shrug. I do hate her, but there's no use in her knowing that, and besides, I hate everyone. When it's spread so thin like that, the hate, is it really anything at all? We're kind of stuck with each other.

"You going to talk or are you back to being mute?" she says. "It's super hard work doing the talking for two. Usually I don't have to. My brother and my mum fill up the silences, you know? I'm the quiet one! But I guess that won't work out with you." She pauses, runs her finger around the edge of a card, then flips it over. "Okay, well. Um. Let's talk about sports. You like the Yankees? Is that a New York thing? The Yankees? Come on, give me a break, okay? I won't tell if you talk. Maybe you could whisper." She whispers the last part, which makes me shiver. I've read on the Internet about people dialing up YouTube videos, listening to people whispering, and right up till this second, I thought that was totally crazy. Now I'm not so sure. I raise my eyebrow at her, and she whispers, "You do know how to whisper, right?" Goose bumps. I rub my arms. Screw this. I raise my hand in the Official Sharkboy Goodbye and head down the steps to the beach, tripping a couple of times because this is a whole new kind of darkness to me. Nothing is even. Everything is off balance.

Kelby, Kelby, Kelby, I think out loud in my head, so maybe she can hear me. Maybe she'll follow me. Maybe I want her to.

Maybe I don't.

The tide is high, so I find a rock and sit on it, take off my shoes, and let my feet rest in the water, which is as cold as ice.

She really is stupidly beautiful, which is pretty unfair. I mean, any guy would be interested. She doesn't look anything like Daff, but she reminds me of Daff, because everything and everyone reminds me of Daff, from the barnacles that are poking my calves to the lump of seaweed floating slightly too far away to reach.

My phone buzzes, startling me. It's easy to forget about your phone when you are here, on a rock, on an island, mosquitoes feasting on your arms. I wrestle it out of my pocket, almost dropping it into the water by my feet, catching it just in time.

Wnt to hear a rddle? LMK. Daff.

I type back, *Non. Rien est drôle.*

I'm smiling though. What is wrong with me? The King is dead. There shouldn't be smiling or summer air or the smell of the ocean or the show-off stars up there and all this crazy beauty because it's all wrong.

I turn the phone off. I turn it back on. I text him. *Want to hear a riddle? Let me know.* Send. The fact that it doesn't bounce back is such a relief that I exhale something that was stuck without realizing I'd been holding my breath.

"Girlfriend?" She startles me, Kelby, suddenly standing in front of me, teetering on a loose log. It wobbles and she hops off. "I always text so much when I first get here but then after I've been here for a while, it kind of seems less important, you know? Like I actually don't care what anyone over there"—she waves her hand in the direction of Vancouver—"is doing, you know? I probably should, but I don't. It feels like a different life or like, I don't know, a movie. This party or that party or so-and-so did this or here is a picture of some idiot puking in a bucket or she said what? To who? I mean, I *really* don't care."

I have a perfect view of the smooth brown skin on her knees. I look away, embarrassed.

"You should probably know that I have a boyfriend," she says.

"I see you falling in love with my knees right now. I'm not blind. And he's a big guy. He could take you out." She laughs. "Enh, screw that. Does anyone actually fight about girls anymore? I *do* have a boyfriend, but he's small. Well, not *small*. He's normal. He's a normal guy with normal friends who is doing who-cares-what in Vancouver right now and I just . . . don't care. I should care! But I don't care." She pauses and stares up at the sky. "Holy crap, those stars. Right? Maybe it's just that . . . none of this matters. Not really. What he's doing. Why I'm not texting him. Why I'm telling you this while you sit there like a big dope and stare at my knees." She shrugs. "Tide's coming in, let's go up."

I follow her up the stairs and she lies down on the hammock and I hesitate, but she pats the spot next to her, like sure, yes, it's obvious that I'm invited to lie with her. Getting in is awkward and I nearly tip us out. Finally, I'm in and I can feel the whole length of her body next to me and I try to pretend to myself that I'm not noticing it but come on, of course I'm noticing it.

She starts talking again like she never stopped, like the whole interlude of getting up the steps and into the hammock didn't happen. "He's actually probably going to dump me at the end of the summer, if he hasn't already. But that's okay. He's normal. He's a normal guy who likes, I don't know, soccer and video games and drinking and doing stupid stunts with his friends and whatever normal people do. Normal is so boring. You know? No. I don't know either. Normal can be good, I guess. I think if you were normal, you'd have different expectations. If you were normal, you'd be disappointed less often. I basically wasn't in love with him, but I kinda had a crush on *normal*. Do you know what I mean? I don't think I know about love, not really. It seems stupid, but then I see my mum and your dad and . . ." She pauses. "I guess that's weird for you, if he didn't mention it. Men are such idiots, actually."

I want to ask her why she thinks she isn't normal, because from where I'm lying, she's the only normal person around. But my voice isn't willing to play along, the inside of my mouth is sand and seaweed and the ocean and the tide, but it isn't making words. Not yet. Not right now.

"Talking around you is exhausting, it turns out," she says, stretching. "I'm going to quit. If you don't answer, I don't talk. I've already said way too much. Shooting star!"

I've missed it, but I look up anyway. We lie in silence for a while, our breathing synching, which is nice. The night is freckling up with stars, more stars than I've ever seen. I get caught up in looking at those stars but I don't forget she's there, warm and present beside me. She smells like sunscreen and something sweet: honey or vanilla or cake. Do all girls smell like cupcakes? What is it with that? Do they do it on purpose? As it gets darker, more and more stars appear, so that it looks like there is star dust behind the star fragments behind the stars themselves. It's flat-out amazing.

"At least half those stars are probably ghosts, if you think about it," she says suddenly. "That's maybe partly why I'm so into them. The stars. And ghosts. Listen. Think about this: a lot of them have already burned out, they aren't even *there* right now. But we can see them like they are there. We see them, so they exist, right? But they don't! They are long gone! Mind-blowing, right? There is nothing actually there, only dark space. So if you think about it"—her voice speeds up—"why is it so weird that some people can see *people* that are gone? Like ghosts? Why is it so strange to imagine that they leave a mark? Like it's taking longer than normal for the fact of their death to travel to our eyes? Do you believe in that kind of stuff? I guess you aren't going to answer. But you could nod. Or *something*. God, this is sort of annoying, Snort. I wish you'd say something."

I try to speak. I want to say something, but my voice is gone again, a crackling dead leaf where a sound should be. I cough instead. *Crackle crackle.* I nod, shrug, shake my head. Do I believe in ghosts? Would I want to?

No. Yes. I don't know.

"Sorry," she says. "I get a little . . . Mum says I'm overly imaginative. Which is good, because I'm a writer. I'm going to be a writer. I'm writing a book. About the stars and stuff. When I say it like that, it doesn't sound good. But it is. I like it, anyway. Probably no one else will ever read it. Maybe you'll want to."

I smile, as much as I can. Because I do want to, actually. I want to read Kelby's book.

"If you laugh at me, I'm going to—"

I laugh a little bit, and she raises her hand and punches me in the arm, which hurts more than I would have thought, so I move quick and the hammock flips, spilling us out on the deck in a tangle of arms and legs and bodies. Which is nice, honestly. Except for the bruising.

"Shit!" she yells from under me.

Charlie sits bolt upright on the couch. "You swore!" he says. "I'm going to tell Mum. You're going to get it."

Kelby crawls away, gets up, dusting off her knees. (She's right about her knees, I am in love with them. Maybe. A little bit, anyway.)

"Charlie," she says. "If you tell, then I am *not* taking you out tomorrow. Or ever. *Never*. Got it? Just don't. I will put a spider in your bed, kid, I swear."

"Okay, okay," he says amiably. "Hey, can *I* swear?"

"No," she says. "You're too young."

"Then I'll tell," he says, sort of sadly. "I'm not really scared of spiders anyway."

"Okay, fine," she says. "But just once."

"*Fuck*," he says, looking really pleased with himself. "Wooo-hoo! Stupid! Shit!"

"Stop," she says. "Time's up."

He grins. One of his teeth is broken off at the bottom, making him look like a hapless kid from an old 1950s sitcom. He runs down the stairs and scrambles up an arbutus tree that curves out from the bank, hanging low over the beach below.

"His favorite tree," she tells me. "Mum gets weird when we swear. She's kind of religious," she adds. "I'm not. In case you're wondering."

I nod again. The nodding is getting boring and I really want to talk and I hate that nothing comes out, that my voice is blocked off by the lump that's always in my throat, and here I am in the middle of nowhere in this surreal place with a girl—a pretty girl—and I'm mute. Dumb. Useless.

And she's right about the stars. Most of them are long gone, yet there they are, shining through the tiny pinprick holes in the whole big stupid universe.

"Sorry," I whisper.

But I don't think she hears me. The word is too small, a feather on my tongue and the wind blows it away before it makes a sound.

24

THE NEXT MORNING, THE SKY IS A WHITE-GRAY HAZE
of heat and the air is still. Even the trees seem to have rolled up
their shadows, leaving the ground painfully exposed. Instead of
being warm, the sandstone burns my bare feet. Sunlight glares
through the glass, the reflections stab my eyes like blades.

Dad is worried about fire. "This whole island could go up like
a giant bonfire," he says. "Let's go up to the site."

I walk with him up the steep trail to where the hotel's founda-
tion looks like it was dropped from outer space. It doesn't fit here.
The salal is growing over it like it is trying to reclaim its space. Moss
creeps up the support beams. Lichen. Stuff I can't name. I'd ask
Dad, but I'm not sure I want to get him started. Blackberry brambles
are hugging some low walls like they are stretching to see over the
top. Predictably, the unfinished building reminds me of all the other
unfinished buildings, which takes me right back to the forty-second
floor. Whoopee. I brace myself for the ride. My stomach clenches.

Then, nothing.

Or at least, a wave of nausea, but nothing more. I clear my throat. I think of The King, lying in his coffin, neatly, like he did on the ground beside the roller coaster, but of course, he's not lying like that in his coffin. He's in pieces.

He's fallen apart.

Now I'm dizzy.

Now I feel it.

It's like poking a bruise, pressing harder and harder, making sure it still hurts.

Pink mist.

I gag, and spit into the bush.

"You okay?" says Dad.

I nod, lying. Yes, no, I will never be okay again.

I pull my phone out of my pocket and type, *pink mist*. Then I delete it. I don't have anyone to send that to. I don't have any way of explaining. I take a picture of my bare feet on the path and send it to Mom. *Swoooooop, swooooooop,* all the way to Antwerp, where the show's hero will try to woo the women by making them bungee jump from a famous landmark and pose in front of tourist attractions in their bikinis, blinking up at him and crying into the camera about love. What do they know about love? I loved The King. I love Daff.

But actually, I don't know anything about love, either. I shiver, thinking about the hammock last night and Kelby lying next to me and all those stars.

Dear Sharkboy, wear shoes! You're going to get athlete's foot. Love, Mom, she writes. I grin.

It's not a public pool, I type. *It's the freaking forest.* Then I delete it. *Love you, too, Mom.* I send it and pocket the phone. She won't answer. She answers once, and then that's it. The conversation is over. She has abs to delineate with airbrush tools, after all.

I take a photo of Dad, sweating through his shirt ahead of me, the sun glaring down on his bald spot, which practically *twinkles* in the light, and send it to The King. *Spray hair in can, it's what's for Father's Day*, I type. *LOL*.

Then I miss him so hard I have to stop for a minute. Bend over. Pretend to brush something off my foot, the pain deep in my stomach like a fist.

I saw a movie once where the people in the film got to take a pill and it would erase a person from their memory entirely and every memory associated with that person. If I could do that, would I? I think maybe I would. I would lose a lot, but then I'd be free because seriously, my hands are shaking and my breath is rasping and I am thinking of the words I don't want to think of *death love decomposing*, a trifecta of Things I Don't Want to Think About. Not now, not ever. So I do the only thing I can think of and that is to start to climb. I pull myself up the timber frame.

"Hey," Dad says. "Careful there, kiddo. It ain't a jungle gym." He looks around. "Though it's not much good for anything else, I guess," he mutters. He reaches for a beam, does a couple of pull-ups. He's not in bad shape, for a dad. "Feels good!" he says. "I should do this more often."

I look away, blinking. Sweat and everything pouring into my eyes and stinging. Who said my dad could be *fun*? Who said my dad could be *normal*?

The wood of the building is hot and dry because everything has become hot and dry. I center myself over a beam and wobble. Only ten feet off the ground and the vertigo has grabbed me tight. I try to remember why I liked that feeling. I try to remember how to find my center. I try. Everything is trying. There is nothing but trying.

What did The King's dad used to say? Oh, yeah. *There is no try, there is only do, you fucking imbecile.*

I force myself to concentrate. Ahead of me there is a gap of maybe five feet before the building continues. A wider timber on what was obviously going to be a grand ceiling. The dining room maybe? The wide timber is twelve inches wide, which—in parkour—is a joke. It's not even hard. To jump from this beam to that. It's like parkour for preschoolers. Anyone could do it.

But can I?

I do a lap around the beam structure that I'm standing on. It's wobbly but I try to trust. Everything about parkour is obvious when you're doing it, the moves rush at you in the split second before you perform them. The secret is not hesitating. *He who hesitates is lost,* Mr. Bills in English Lit class wrote on the wall in black Sharpie. Then beside it in red, with an arrow pointing back at the quote, *#truefact.*

I make my focus smaller. I feel the wood under my feet, the air on my face. *#justbe* I don't look at my dad, who is digging something in the ground around the back of the building. The structure itself is small except in this context, it's huge. In New York, this would be tiny. But here, in the woods, it looks like a behemoth. And building this without roads or power or machinery seems ridiculous and impossible, like the pyramids or the Notre Dame Cathedral or Easter freakin' Island.

Some of the beams I am lightly running on now aren't level. A few buckle in the middle from age—this thing was started a bunch of years ago—and probably because they were built wrong to begin with and maybe because the island itself is rejecting it, pushing the building off itself. *Abscissing* it. I climb up, the highest point being only about twenty feet of skeletal structure but right away I'm dizzy and I drop back down, a quick flip to the ground, my heart hammering.

Maybe this kind of thing isn't fun for me anymore. Maybe it never will be again. And anyway, it's something guys do together, not one guy alone.

One guy alone just looks stupid, cartwheeling on a splintering timber, his hands slivered and slick with sweat.

But I have to. That's the thing. I've got to do it, for no other stupid reason than because I can't give this one to The King. He doesn't get to take this with him.

I climb back on.

I run.

"Hey," says Dad. "You're going to fall, kiddo. No hospitals here, you know."

(And there I am again, "Hey, Chief Not Scared of Heights, you're going to fall." And that *what*, stretching so thin, like jungle vines that will never reach the ground.)

I jump.

My hands flap at the air, like they can keep me up. Feathers now, I think. There aren't feathers. Well, duh.

I miss, but not by much. Enough that I can grab the beam with my hand, splinters ripping into my palms before I drop off, wiping them on my shorts, pretending that's what I meant to do.

Dad stares at me. "Kids these days," he says. "I guess I'm getting old because that just looked idiotic to me. I'd ask if you were okay, but I guess you are, if this is what you do for fun." He shakes his head. "When did I become such an old man?" He raises his fist to the heavens and mock shouts, *"Git off my lawn, kid!"*

I grin, in spite of how I really feel. My hands are burning. There's a sliver or something in my foot that is throbbing with every beat of my heart.

"Nothing we can do anyway," Dad says. "About the fire risk, I mean. Hope it rains. But maybe if this thing burns down then insurance will get paid out and everyone will be happy. But then I'd be unemployed. Hey, did I tell you about this thing here called squatters' rights? It's when . . ."

I nod, not listening. Sometimes it's hard to focus on his voice, it's like my thoughts crowd him out and even though I know he's talking, I can't quite grab on to the words. Overhead, an eagle soars low and proud, landing in a tree. Staring at us. Waiting for something to happen. He's close enough for me to see his eyes, hooked yellow beak, talons made for tearing. Zeus growls and the bird takes off, rising into the air like he's mocking me and the way gravity pulls me down again and again and again.

"Yeah," says Dad. "Anyway, I don't know. I don't know sometimes why I'm in charge of this. If it starts to burn, then what? I'm going to call for help and then get out. This whole forest would go up, just like that." He snaps his fingers. "Most of the time this job is the best, but now it's pure stress. Man." He shakes his head.

I don't meet his eye. This? This is stressful? It's not even a job, not really. He's a placeholder. He does . . . nothing.

A small forest of moss sprawls under our feet. A squirrel darts up a tree and chuckles at us. The eagle changes his mind about landing again and soars away in the other direction. I wonder how long it will be before the squirrel is his lunch. Do eagles eat squirrels? They must, right?

I turn to head back to the cabin, when Dad says, "Hey, you know, Darcy has a lot of . . . She's pretty interesting. She's a person you might like. I don't know how . . . I mean, obviously this is awkward, and I didn't tell you about her, but I didn't quite know how. But you and she have a lot in common. More than you think. She was thinking you might want to go out with them this afternoon. She's really . . . spiritual. I know I'm not, but maybe she can help you with your . . ."

I wait, eyebrows raised.

"Diving," he finishes. "They—we—dive for scallops and sell them so they can afford to stay here for the entire summer. She can show you the best dive. If you want. I know you've got your— you can borrow my stuff. I have some editing to do anyway. Someone found a mistake in *The Greatest Adventure of Our Time #6*. I've gotta fix that."

I nod, fast. Yes. Yes, I want to dive. Yes. But also, something twists in my gut. My dad dives? And he never thought to mention it? The *one* thing we might have in common? How clueless can any man be?

I will never understand him. I shift my weight from one side to the other and then, wanting to get away, I raise my hand and start to run back down the steep path. Faster than he can keep up with. Faster than I knew I could go. ("You should be on the track team,"

Coach Smithers said, back at school. "You're a star, kid." Something The King would never let go. "You're a star, kid," he'd mimic. "You're a shootin' star, I'd wager.")

Back at the cabin, I easily scale the trunk of the tree that Charlie was on yesterday. Past where he went. Past where I should go. The tree curves up and then down like a tipped letter *C*, its uppermost branches pointing back down to the beach. The trunk of the tree is solid and cool under my touch, the red papery bark of it peeling away easily. I concentrate on not slipping. When I finally stop, I am too high. The highest. Higher than I should be. Down on the beach, I see Charlie and his bucket.

"Hi!" he shouts. *"Hi, you are up my tree!"*

I nod even though he can't see me, and swing myself partway down on the branches, arm over arm, like a monkey. Then, without thinking, I do a flip and land on the ground beside him. It's a long enough drop that my feet reverberate with the impact and the pain ripples up my legs and back like the aftershock of an earthquake. His eyes are wide. "Holy cow," he says. "That was cool. Can I do it?"

I shake my head hard. *No. It's too dangerous.*

I point at his fish to distract him. In the white of the bucket, six or seven tiny fish are darting behind a piece of seaweed that floats on the surface. The water in that bucket has to be hot. Too hot. I point at the tide pool and then at the bucket.

"I'm *going* to put them back," he says. "I was building them a camp. So they could have a holiday. From their regular place. They probably like it, huh?"

"Hot," I whisper.

"Hey," he says. "I knew you could talk." He sticks his finger in the bucket. "Yeah," he adds. "It's hot."

He picks the bucket up and tips it, the fish and water and seaweed slopping out in too much of a rush into the tide pool. One fish doesn't make it, lands stunned on the hot rock instead. I flick it into the water. It probably won't survive, but still, I couldn't leave it there like that. Exposed. Dying. Hopeless. It floats for a second and then disappears under some seaweed. I will it to swim. *Come on, little guy. Flick that tail.*

Dad finally bursts through the trees. "Oh, there you are!" he says. "You move fast. Man, I need to start running again."

Charlie rolls his eyes. "He's old, huh," he whispers.

I laugh, inasmuch as I can. Then, sort of as an afterthought, I take my phone out of my pocket and snap a photo of Dad, bent over, clutching his side, his T-shirt drenched with sweat. *My old old man,* I type. My finger hovers over the Send button, and then I fire it off to The King, the shadow pigeons swooping it to his grave, where what remains of him is going, going, gone.

I read on the Internet somewhere how the weight of the dirt shoveled back into the grave collapses most coffins. The King's won't collapse though. Maybe not ever. Maybe he'll remain intact forever, reclining on his royal satin sheets, a small fake mortician-made smile playing at the corner of what is left of his lips, an Egyptian king with his most prized treasures, preserved forever.

But then again, nothing about the way The King died left him intact, did it?

25

THE WATER HAS A LOOSE CHOP TO IT AND TODAY IS
blue-gray flecked with those silver sprinkles scattered generously
by the sun, gentler than yesterday, but still so dry. Dad's scuba
stuff fits me perfectly but it feels like I've put on someone else's
skin and it's sticking to me in all the wrong places, in all the wrong
ways.

I'm trying not to hyperventilate before I'm even in the water,
trying to remember everything I learned, hoping I don't panic and
flail and embarrass myself. It feels like forever ago that I did this
the last time, and from here my recollection of it is as hazy as a
dream.

The boat rocks on the choppy waves. Kelby is readying to go
into the water first. She looks so hot in that wet suit and my eyes
can't find anywhere to land without making me feel like I'm perv-
ing out on her. I settle on her face, but her eyes unnerve me, the
way she stares back, unblinking. "Hiya, Snort," she said when she
saw me. "What's shaking? Here's the deal. I won't mention ghosts

today. Swearsies, swearsies, double swearsies on a soldier. Is that a saying? I don't even know half the time if something is a thing or if it's something weird that Mum made up when we were little. Being a mum must be awesome. You could teach your kids anything! You could teach them a bunch of lies, right, *Mum*?" She gives her mom a look.

"What?" says Darcy.

"Forget it," says Kelby.

I nod, staring staring staring. Her hair looks like the down of a baby bird, waving above her skull like that. I mean, that doesn't sound pretty, but trust me, it is. Like feathers.

Charlie drops in a marker to show where she is going in, then she's dangling off the side of the boat like a spider monkey. *Like a spider monkey. Clambering up the roller coaster tracks. Tipping backward off the beam, like a diver.*

I swallow instead of vomiting, try to forget instead of remembering.

Charlie, Darcy, and Kelby have a routine that feels like a conversation I'm interrupting just by being here. I don't belong here. I belong with Daff and The King. I belong on Coney Island. I belong anywhere but here. I rub my eyes so no one can see that I'm about to cry.

Darcy has been filling up the empty spaces with a conversation I don't care about and I can't wait to get into the water to make it stop. She found God, you know, sometime last year, and wants everyone to know. *Look! There he is now, behind that mountain in the distance!* Except that's not God, it's a plane, flying low. She may be the craziest of us all. She sings. Hymns. No kidding, actual hymns, in a crystal-clear voice and as loud as anything. Her voice is probably bouncing along the strait, floating into passing boats, wrapping around the broken souls of strangers. Hell, maybe she is fixing them. Who knows? But not me. I am not fixable and I don't believe in God, at least not that version. And now I only want to get into the water. At the same time, I also want to go to shore, claim a stomachache, hide out in the woods or at the beach and escape. Lie in the hammock, read one of Dad's library of "adventure" books. Cry.

I want to cry.

Again, like on the plane. I want to bawl like a *stupid fucking idiot*, okay?

But I won't. I can't. I take a deep breath. Hold it in.

"You all right?" Darcy says. I nod. Who me? Oh, I'm just peachy. The rolling of the boat is not helping me feel less queasy.

She grins and then, "Well, it's your turn, kid. *Go.*" I adjust everything there is to adjust and hesitate briefly before I tip backward into the sea. Just for a second, the sky cartwheels and the gulls seem to be flying right at me, the clouds twirling and I can't help but think about the fact that the sky flipping like that was what he saw. This same upside down, turn over, and then he was under (or gone) and so am I, with a muffled *whoomp* in my ears, I am under, awkwardly, too heavy, limbless, sinking. I bob for a few seconds, adjusting nothing and then the feeling comes back to me. The thing to do. I slow my breathing and let myself sink. Then I find Kelby and follow her flippers down farther and farther than I would have expected to go.

We are down for as long as we can be. There is no storm that chases us in, there is only us and the reef and the roots of the kelp and more different colors of seaweed than I thought could exist. Purple and red starfish encrust the rocks below the tide line, the seafloor is covered with blue mussels and anemones and fish. This is more like a coral reef than the coral reefs that I saw in the IMAX show about coral reefs. The colors are dizzying and vivid and surreal and it is so beautiful, more beautiful than anything ever has been, and I can feel myself crying behind my mask even as she's pointing to a huge crab, waving one pincher at us as though he wants to float himself up and take a swipe, show who is king.

The King is the king, I tell him silently. I push the water down with my flippers and twirl once or twice. This is what it feels like to be free and alive and I want to whoop and yell and say something and do something and I want him to be *alive* so he can see this, too, and that's too much to ask and I almost throw up, bile rising into the back of my throat.

I hope he saw the colors before he was gone for good. Just for a second, a kaleidoscope of life and light and everything.

I don't want to ever go up, the sun's rays filter through from the surface that is wavering above me, we collect scallops in our bags, filling them up easily and quickly. And then we have to go. It's time.

I don't want to talk about it afterward but weirdly I want to *talk*. It's like my voice has become unstoppered, so as soon as my mouthpiece is out, whatever was blocking me from saying anything is gone, and without even thinking about it, I say, "That was incredible!" I catch a look between Darcy and Kelby but I don't care, and then I'm talking and talking and it's like I can't stop, about everything we saw and the colors and how I wish I had a camera and how it was better than I thought and about sharks and how there aren't very many species here because the water is cold but there are at least seven, including the basking shark, which is basically the coolest-looking shark in the world if you are into that sort of thing, which I am. I tell them about the different kinds of thresher sharks and how even, sometimes, great whites come this far north—farther, even, to Alaska—but not in inland waters, like where we are now, and also, actually, did they see *Sharkwater* because it's a real thing, a real problem, about the food chain and the plankton and the oxygen.

Charlie looks up at me from where he is sitting on the floor of the boat and says, "Seriously, I might have liked you better when you were dumb," and I say, "What?" at the same time as Darcy is saying, "*Charlie*, that is rude!" and he says, "Muuuum, that's what you told me it was called. And he's scaring me."

And I'm like, "Don't be scared. We can do something about it. You can be in my shark army. We can save the sharks!" And he says, "But what if they don't know we are saving them and they bite off our feet?" And I say, "They probably won't." And he says, "That doesn't make me feel better, champ."

Kelby is laughing and laughing.

And Darcy says, "I'm sorry, JC, I don't know what is wrong with these kids."

And we are all talking at once and laughing and it's so normal, like we are normal people who aren't crazy. We don't have ghosts and weirdnesses and a terror that lives in the pit of our stomach, twisting there while it waits to explode outward. We are just people. There are cormorants on the exposed reef, drying their wings, hanging out in a row like babies in Batman costumes; the seals languish in the last of the sun; the bucket is full of scallops; my skin is sweating under the wetsuit, and it's a perfect day.

Perfect.

I help with the boat and then take a quick swim in the bay with Kelby. Finally, I climb back up the stairs to the cabin where Dad is hunched over his laptop typing. I raise my hand to greet him and he says, "How was it?" and instantly, my voice is gone again, my throat feeling like I swallowed gravel. It's not that I don't want to talk, more like it would be impossible even to try.

But it doesn't matter. I don't care. I don't want to tell him. I want to keep today to myself, like a piece of art, like something I've created for only me.

And Kelby, I guess.

And Charlie.

And I guess even for Darcy.

But not Dad. Not yet. I'm just not ready for that.

26

I GO UPSTAIRS AND PICK UP MY PHONE. IT FEELS WRONG,
weird somehow. Foreign. Like an alien object that doesn't belong
here. But I can't help it. It's such a habit. I text Daff. I type, *"Le
tout est magnifique sous le Salish Sea."*

Then I delete it. Actually, I delete her whole conversation, so
the top of my screen says *Daff* and then the entire screen is pure
unadulterated whiteness. None of her begging to talk to me. None
of my French nonanswers. Only nothingness.

The void.

Which is kind of what I believe death is like. *Is it?* I ask The
King silently. *Is that it?* I type, *Can you hear me now, caller?* and
send it to him. Even the *swoop* sounds slow and bored with my at-
tempt, carrying my message into the ether.

But right away, the phone vibrates and she's there. *Lstn, Shrk,
I don't care if U nvr talk 2 me agn. But read yr mail, kk?*

I type *unsubscribe,* and hit Send. I'm too lazy to Google what
that is in French.

FU, she responds.

I take a picture out the window. It's perfect. The tide is starting to run, so you can see whirlpools skimming the surface of the pass outside the window, a few small boats bobbing there, people fishing for salmon in the current. The little rocky beach is empty, Charlie's tree splaying a perfect shadow of itself onto the ground. I don't bother with filters. I hit Send and the pigeons swoop.

And right away, a response buzzes. At first I think it's her.

But it doesn't say Daff.

It says, *The King.*

And I think, for that split second, that somehow he's made it work, texting from the marble tomb.

But that's not it.

It's nothing.

Only a blank.

My own message bouncing back or maybe for real this time, it's over. There's nowhere for it to go. Maybe his phone is decomposing, too, disintegrating in what is left of him.

I curl over, like I've been struck.

"No," I say out loud. *"NO."*

I grab my phone and throw it hard into the corner of the room where it breaks a huge cobweb and then falls to the floor. The glass cracks and I leave it there, faceup, the jagged glass looking like how I feel, ruined beyond all repair.

I mean, I knew he wasn't getting the messages. Of course he wasn't.

It's just that I sort of thought he was.

I needed to send them.

I needed them to land.

And right away, the beautiful day turns ugly and I am alone on a lumpy single bed with stupid Spider-Man sheets and three dogs that are too big for the space, wondering why I'm here and what I'm supposed to do next.

21

HERE IS WHAT I DO NEXT:

I get up in the morning.

I walk with the dogs.

I swim with Kelby.

I talk less.

And less.

I dive more.

And more.

And inside, I feel like my tinfoil heart is crumpling harder and harder into a tighter and tighter ball, so that even if you could reinflate it, it would be so damaged, you'd hardly recognize it as being the heart it once was.

I walk more.

I swim more.

I slowly am becoming the island. I imagine becoming the island. I visualize my arms and legs becoming trees, my torso hardening to sandstone, my mind flying off the reef with a cormorant, black wings against the blue sky.

The skin on my feet is like leather.

I climb trees and swing from branches.

I think about staying.

Never going back.

I think about that a lot.

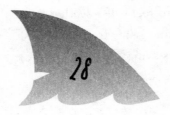

28

Dear Daff,

This is the first time I have opened my laptop in two whole weeks. It's dusty.

I feel like you won't forgive me.

I feel like you shouldn't.

I haven't read your stupid attachment yet, if that's what you're wondering.

I am in a weird place right now. In my head. And also, literally. I mean, places like this don't really exist, yet here I am.

Maybe I time traveled, like the hero in Dad's book, jumping through time and space to come to a place that can't exist, yet does.

The Internet doesn't belong here.

Nothing does, least of all me.

But here I am.

It all makes me think of the word bisect.

My life was bisected. *I've been thinking about words a lot. About* abscission. *Have you ever heard that word? It means something about how the trees get their leaves off in the fall, like a dog shaking them free. Sort of. I think about how The King's dad's stupid building abscised him. Right? Does that make sense to you? It's like his whole life, his dad was trying to shake him off, and then at the end, it literally happened. And I can't figure out how to feel about that.*

There was before *and now there is* after, *and they are so different that it feels like everything was a dream anyway and it wasn't real and right now, this is more real than that, but when I get home, that will be more real than this.*

Is it like that for you, too? Is this just temporary?

I broke my phone a couple weeks ago and I haven't missed it.

I broke my phone a couple weeks ago and I've missed your texts so much.

I broke my phone a couple weeks ago.

It's not like there's a place here to get a new phone. It's not like I could afford it if there was.

There are no stores. Nothing. We have to go into town one of these days because there is no milk and the only kind of cereal we have left is cornflakes, and without milk those are basically like eating wood chips.

I wonder how you'd be here. I feel like the island would change around you and you'd stay you, you'd still be Daff. Remember that time we went "camping" on Long Island? And it wasn't even camping and the cabins were nicer than

*any house, but still. We roasted marshmallows on that
beach fire until one of the sparks flew up and landed in
your hair and we got sand in our pants and everywhere and
no one died. I feel like I flip through our memories and look
for the ones where no one died, because that's all of them, I
guess. Except the last one. And that one eclipses the rest.*

I've been really busy.

That's why I haven't written.

*Mostly I get up in the morning and walk the dogs to the
beach. If the tide is right, I swim out to this raft and sit in
the sun on this chair that is out there. It's a yellow Adirondack
chair. It is exactly the same color as the table in the kitchen
at home. It makes me miss my mom and feel guilty about
my phone, which she can't afford to replace, and anyway,
neither can I. Maybe The King's dad can pay for it.*

That's a joke, but it isn't a good one, so forget it.

The other thing I do here is dive.

There's a girl. Her name is Kelby.

There's a girl. I like her.

*There's a girl who I dive with. Her brother is only eight
but he drives the boat and waits for us to come up. That
seems kind of crazy to me, but it works. We go down and
then come up with bags of scallops and every day I see
something unbelievable.*

*Yesterday, I saw an angel shark lying in the sand at the
bottom. Most of the seafloor here is rocky and alive with
barnacles and anemones and seaweed and everything else,
but we dove down and found one patch of sand and in the*

middle something moved, and I nearly choked I was so excited, trying to show Kelby.

The girl's name is Kelby.

Anyway, I'll delete at least half of this and then send none of it.

You know, I'm scared that you're a star that's already burned out, I just haven't seen that yet. You were so much like him. You are so much like him. And both of you are stars, aren't you? As in, famous. But you move differently. You are different. You're brighter.

Are you already gone?

I feel like you are. I wouldn't ever say that for real because it sounds seriously crazy. Medication-level.

I'm scared you're already dead.

Daff.

I'm sorry.

Disregard le tout.

D'accord?

Bon.

Love,

JC

Delete.

29

Dear Daff:

Today, I was diving for scallops with my dad. He does it to help out his girlfriend. She makes her living selling scallops in the summer. In the fall and winter and spring, I guess she's a teacher. She's pretty. You'd like her.

She's nice but she's Christian. I mean, she takes "Christian" to a whole new place. God is everywhere when you're with Darcy. She found Jesus in a potato chip. She sounds like a joke but somehow when she says it, she's so sincere that I want to believe her.

I like her, I guess.

I feel like I should say that.

I feel horrible for my mom when I say that, but it's true. I think Mom still loves him. I think she still doesn't understand why he left. I've been thinking about stuff like that. There's a lot of time for thinking up here. Thinking and walking and swimming and sitting. Yeah. I wonder how

I ever thought about anything before because I don't remember ever feeling like time was this big open thing that I could go into and stay in.

He never mentions her. Dad never mentions Mom.

It's weird how someone can stay so present for one person and just be gone—poof—for another.

Kelby and I do most of the diving and get the scallops. We're getting braver. We're exploring farther and farther.

Kelby knows a lot about the stars. When she explains it, it makes sense for a minute or two. Stuff about the galaxy that I've never thought about. Then I try to think about it afterward, and I can't make it make sense anymore.

Anyway, she was busy. Or asleep. Or spending the day lying on a rock reading a novel about someone who was doing something. Or looking after Charlie, her brother, and our three dogs: Maximus and Apollo and Zeus.

Or

Okay, I don't know what she was doing and it doesn't matter.

Okay, I do know what she was doing. Her boyfriend was here. People who come here who aren't supposed to be here stand out, intrusions in a scene where they don't belong. He was awkward and clumsy. I laughed when he slipped on a wet patch of green seaweed that papered the rock where he jumped. He cut his knee and she gave me a look like she hoped I'd die.

But then she winked and grinned.

But you don't want to know about Kelby.

161

But I'm not sending this, so it doesn't matter.

Nothing matters.

Hey, what do you get when you cross a chicken with a goat?

Forget it.

Anyway, that's not what I wanted to tell you.

I have to tell you about the whales.

You were the first person I wanted to tell.

I wasn't wearing a wet suit because Dad needed his and I pretended that was okay, but I was freezing. I actually thought I might die from how cold it was, except not really. Do you find you do that, too? Hesitate when you say, "God, I thought I'd die"? Because now it means so much more, and eff that, no one ever died from cold water. Although, I guess people have.

I liked the feeling of the water on my skin. This will sound stupid, thus guaranteeing I won't hit Send, but it made me feel like I belonged there. Like I was a shark or a fish or a seal. I could have been anything, part of the ocean. We're all part of our own life cycle, right? But somehow the ocean life cycle makes more sense to me. It fits me better.

I don't know why.

Ashes to ashes, dust to dust. It sounds so dry.

That rhymed. I'd rap it for you if you were here.

I'm glad you're not here.

I wish you were here.

I wished you were here when . . .

I seriously wish I could forget you even existed. If you don't exist, then neither did he.

But whatever. That's not what I wanted to say.

We were diving. Me and Dad.

It was almost time to go up, mostly because I was getting seriously cold. Then I heard this sound that was like nothing I could ever imagine having heard before, yet I knew what it was because it was obvious. Do you ever recognize something you've never heard before? The clicks and whistles. Dad started gesturing at me like crazy, pointing at the surface. I looked up. Passing between me and the sky were three whales. They were so big, Daff. They were so real and present and alive. I don't think you can imagine what that's like, looking up from underneath at the belly of an orca, like they were flying and I was the one underwater. They didn't stop or look at us. They didn't dive down and touch us with their fins. There wasn't some kind of magical freaking Hallmark moment of understanding between us or anything like that. They didn't even seem to notice us. They were simply passing by, perfectly black and white, blocking out the light for only a few seconds, their spray sprinkling the surface with a cloak of fine white bubbles.

It was the most everything I have ever seen. The everyanything.

Remember that poem?

You loved it.

I guess I thought it was dumb, but I kind of get it now.

I'm more like my dad than I would have thought. The whole thing didn't make me feel like I understood the whales, it made me feel like I understood him. Dad. Because when we got to the surface, he started to cry. Then he said, "I don't know why I'm crying, but I can't stop. Holy crap, that was amazing. That was amazing." Then he just went ahead and cried, like that was an okay thing to do.

I think maybe my dad is a good man after all.

When we came back in on the boat, every one of the seals was gone from the reef. They know when the whales are coming through and they disappear for days, Dad says.

I'm the seal.

You're the whale.

We're all the seals.

We're all the whales.

Dad dropped me at the raft in the middle of the bay and I sat in the yellow chair in the sinking sun until I stopped shivering.

The dumb part was that I then had to swim in. Now I'm cold again. My hands are shaking, typing this.

What are you doing right now?

Are you over him?

I want you to walk down the block where it happened. I want you to look at the sidewalk and see if you can see the mark. See if it's still there. How does that work? Does someone have to bleach it away? Scrub it clean?

That job would suck.

I miss you.

I don't miss you.

This place is amazing.

Those whales. Seriously.

Love,

JC

30

"HE'S GONE, YOU KNOW," SAYS KELBY. SHE IS SPRAWLED
out on the reef next to me, like a seal, absorbing the heat. Except
she's a pretty seal in a hot bikini.

A pretty seal in a hot bikini who has a boyfriend with a mashed-
in nose who looks like a human pug puppy, who has finally packed
up his tent and gone back to the city. When she was around him,
she was different. She drank beer and belched and laughed too hard
and touched him too much. I wanted to say, *Look, you can like
him, but you don't have to* be *him*. But I didn't want her to like him.
He was such a *regular* guy. He was so average, it hurt. *Normal*. I
totally got what she meant once I met him, with his broad smiling
face and farmer's tan. Even the way he swam, too much splashing,
interrupting the water. He threw himself into the bay and expected
the water to hold him up.

"What?" I say, even though I heard her. My voice still tastes
strange to me, metallic and robotic.

I splash my feet in the water, risking the backs of my calves being maimed by barnacles. The splashes are sending out widening rings that ripple the surface. In the sky, a few puffed-up clouds look like they are playing a part in a kids' cartoon. The heat wave has loosened its grip, finally. Yesterday it poured rain all day, making the whole island seem almost like the only place in the world. The rain erased Vancouver and most of the Salish Sea and the fire risk and the mood that had gripped Dad of resignation. He was freaking elated. A bullet dodged. The place can't burn when it's wet.

A gray haze hung everywhere. The hammering of the rain on the roof sounded like something I'd only ever imagined until I heard it, then I felt like I'd been hearing it all my life. Now, instead of being stifling hot, it's perfect, scrubbed clean. The air hangs easy in the sky, warm and fresh. The water is cold and clear.

"We broke up," she says, blowing a bubble with gum I didn't know she was chewing.

"Oh yeah?" I say. My voice is too heavy for my mouth. "Great," I add. I stand up. Stretch tall, toward the wispy clouds. I hesitate for a second. "Hope you're okay," I add. Then I dive under the water, let it fill up my ears and my mouth and my nose. One sharp breath in and it would be in my lungs. Then what?

Then nothing.

Then I would be nothing.

Then everything would be nothing.

I open my eyes and spin my body over, like a seal. Through the distorted surface, I can see her standing on the rock, waiting to jump in. I swim hard and fast out into the middle of the bay, my muscles feel strong and hurt just enough for me to keep going, still on that same held breath. You can go a long way on one inhalation, it turns out.

I climb out at the raft, sit in the chair for a while. She's sat back down, didn't come after me. I feel disappointed and relieved at the same time. From here, it looks like she's reading and I miss her. What is wrong with me?

Daff, I think. But I'm trying to think of her. She's fading, that's the problem. Daff and my feelings for her, what's happening to them? Can meeting just one new girl completely erase the old one? What kind of guy am I, anyway?

I lean back and pick at the yellow paint on the arms of the chair and I miss my mom and I miss The King and I try and try and try and try to remember how it felt to be New York–me, and not island-me, and it's fading, like the yellow of this stupid chair in the sun.

I belly flop back into the water and the surface slaps my stomach hard. Stinging. I swim hard and messy, with arms like Kelby's boyfriend, flapping and splashing me to the shore, like a bird with a broken wing, beating uselessly at the air.

I finally climb back up next to Kelby, my muscles shaking from the effort.

"Did I tell you that Mum once took me to this priest friend of hers and he did an actual exorcism?" she says, like we're in the middle of a conversation. "He for real laid his hands on my head and screamed things in Latin. Then he moved his hands. Actually"—she lowers her voice—"I think he copped a feel."

I stare at her, blinking salt water from my eyes.

"I know, right?" she asks.

"Wow," I say, finally. "That's intense."

Two kayakers in bright yellow boats slide by on the glassy sea. *"Nice day!"* one shouts. I raise my hand. Yes, it's a nice day, sir. Now move it along.

She shrugs. "She thought I was possessed because I kept having nightmares. But you know what? People have nightmares. It's normal." She stops. "Maybe Mum wanted to get the normal out of me?"

"What's up with your mom anyway?" I say to her. "She's pretty over-the-top with the church . . . stuff." Around the back of their cabin, Darcy has been building a little church. An actual church, out of stone. It's tiny, like a playhouse. She goes in there and kneels. She puts flowers on the altar.

Kelby sighs. "I don't really want to talk about it. Can't we talk about something else? Like, I don't know, the first amazing concert you ever saw. Or . . . I don't know. Anything."

"Okay," I say. "It was Foo Fighters, last September, Madison Square Garden." I lean back on the hot rock. It was with Daff and The King. Daff held my hand, so we wouldn't get separated, she said. But it wasn't that. The way she ran her finger around in a circle on my palm. I'd thought it meant something and I'd gone in for the kiss and she'd laughed and said, "No." Not in a mad way, just casually, like that. "No." So I stopped. Then The King came back from getting drinks, three huge cups of Coke spilling out of the drink tray, and then the band started playing, and that was it. That was all of it. The way she held my hand, I thought about that for a long time after. But it didn't mean anything, after all.

"I saw them," Kelby says. "In Vancouver. They weren't that great."

"They were okay. But this rock is great," I say. "I love this rock."

"Weirdo," she says. "It's a rock. There are miles of rock. This whole island is rock."

"This rock is the best rock," I say. "Of all the rocks. I don't know. It's like . . . perfect. It's got this groove thing to lie in. And it's the warmest. And the view! Look at the view!" I wave my arm at the bay, at the sky.

She sighs and lies back. Takes her gum out and sticks it in one of the finger holes in the sandstone. Closes her eyes. Opens them. Sits up.

"A bird could choke to death on that," I say. "You could be committing actual bird homicide with that gum." I pick the gum out and stick it on my shoe.

"Gross," she says.

"I'll throw it out later," I say.

"No bird would eat that," she says. "Birds are smarter than that."

"You think they are," I say. "But what if it's one really stupid bird? What if that one dumb bird that you don't know exists swoops down and is drawn to the delightful pinkness of this gum and then . . . *Bam.* Dead."

"Okay, okay," she says, but she's laughing. "Keep my gum, dude."

"I'm going to," I say. "I am a hero to birds. I am a hero to the *entire animal kingdom.*"

"Right," she says. "We'll talk when you save a hippo from marauders."

"Fine," I say. "I'll save a hippo. Find me a hippo. I'll save it."

"Okay," she says. "Great." She nudges me. "Hero."

"That's me," I say, suddenly needing to swallow a lump in my throat. "The Great White Hope."

"What?" she says.

"Nothing," I say. "But what were you going to tell me?"

"Oh," she says. "Yeah."

She moves away from me a bit and hangs her feet down the other side of the rock. The tide is starting to cover the sandbar. "We could make an island," she says. "On the sand."

"Nah," I say. "We can make an island tomorrow. Let's just talk."

"Okay," she says. "You know, maybe it was better when you didn't talk."

"Maybe," I say. "I could've been the silent savior of birds with special needs."

"And hippos," she says, but she doesn't laugh.

Then, all at once, "Look, my dad died, okay? My dad died. My dad . . . died. He died and Mom found God and I found . . ." Her voice falters. "I found the stars. I figured out what they meant to me. After. I mean, we find the thing that saves us, right? That's what happens. That's the normal thing that happens." She looks up at me, her eyes glistening with tears. "I know that sounds cheesy, so don't you dare make fun of me. Not right now. I'm telling you that my dad died. No jokes allowed."

"Okay," I say carefully. "I'm sorry. I'm really sorry."

"Yeah," she says. "So this is what happened. I'm going to tell you. Don't talk, only listen. This is the whole story: We were in the yard. The backyard behind our apartment building. Our building was an old house, split into apartments. It was nice. It wasn't like an alley out back, it was like a real yard. Grass. The whole bit. Like something out of a storybook. I think that's why they chose the apartment, for that square of grass that made them feel like real proper parents. Dad had this telescope and we were going to watch a meteor shower. He always loved that stuff. It was *his* thing." She stops. Her eyes are slowly leaking, tears pooling on her lips. I know it's entirely the wrong thing to think, but what I'm thinking is that I want to kiss her. "Now it's mine," she added. "Now the stars are mine. So I guess he left me the stars. Pretty nice, right? Better than leaving me a check, I guess." She laughs, but not like it's funny, like she's sad. The saddest.

There's probably something wrong with me that someone is pouring out their heart to me, and I am thinking about kissing. She licks the tear off her top lip. I shiver.

"I'm sorry," I say again. I want there to be something bigger and more meaningful to say, but I can't find the words. *Sorry* feels as weightless as a feather.

"So we were out there," she continues. "And he smoked, right? He was like this *secret* smoker. He thought we didn't know that he smoked but he did smoke and he snuck away behind this shed thing that was back there, for a cigarette, and then there was this—"

She stops. In the distance, one of the dogs is howling. Then a second one joins in. A seaplane flies low overhead and dips its wings. I can hear voices from somewhere, probably a boat. People laughing.

In real life there are always people laughing at the wrong moment. If this was a TV show, someone would edit that out.

"This," I say, helpfully. "There was this . . ."

"Yeah," she says. "There was this explosion. I guess—I mean, I know. I thought that he . . . I was only nine. So I guess, I just assumed—I mean, I thought he was hit by a meteor. Because right before that, there was this shooting star that was huge. I mean, you could see the tail and everything. It stuck in the sky like a tattoo of light. And I was yelling, 'Daddy, did you see—?' and then there was an explosion that blew me into the fence." She holds out her arm and I can see the faint white lines of an old scar, puckering the skin inside her elbow. "His match found a gas leak in the barbecue."

"So he died," she says. "I guess that's the whole story. Except that after that, after the explosion, I saw him. He was standing next to me. He said, 'You're gonna be okay, kid.' He didn't even talk like that, not for real. In real life, he had a British accent. He was English. So he wouldn't have said that. He sounded like John Wayne! My shrink says that's how he knows it's just me, just brain messings, he said. My own brain messing with me. After that, I saw him all the time for a while. And then I stopped seeing him. But I think that it was like seeing a star, you know? You keep seeing its light even though it's already gone."

I wait. "Is 'brain messings' an actual medical diagnosis?" I say.

"Ha ha," she says. "Funny." But she does crack a small smile.

"I'm available for bar mitzvahs, weddings, funerals," I say.

"Gallows humor?" she says.

"Yeah." I nod. "Anyway, I'm sorry."

"Yeah," she says. "Well, people die. You know that, of all people. So the living keep on living and the dead keep on being dead. Right? I guess that's all there is to it."

"I guess," I say.

The tide has risen while we've been talking and my feet are submerged. Under the surface of the water, my feet look distorted and unreal. My heel catches a barnacle and a puff of red clouds out. It doesn't hurt. I'm going to have so many scars from this summer. It's leaving marks all over me. The water is cold. Later, I'll feel it, but for now, it just feels the same as always.

"I guess I wonder if you saw him," she says.

"Who?" I say.

"The King," she says.

"Oh," I say. I swallow. I'm not thinking about kissing anymore. I'm thinking about not throwing up. "No," I say.

She shifts over so her leg is next to mine, our feet are dangling next to each other. Her leg is brown and smooth, mine is whiter and bonier. The place where they are touching is an inferno of heat. Not from the sun.

"Sorry," she says.

"Me too," I manage. "I am, too."

I just want to stop feeling everything. I want it all to stop. I get up, grab my stuff, and head back up to the cabin. I don't look and see if she's still there, but I think she'll probably sit there till it gets dark, waiting to see her dad again up in the stars, and for a minute I'm just so jealous that she has that, she has a place to look. I don't have anything at all.

31

THE DOGS COME RUSHING FROM THEIR USUAL SPOT BEHIND
the logs to greet me and I grab my T-shirt and my pack, which I've
filled with the kind of food that Dad and I still have, which is those
stupid onion chips that he loves, a bag of cornflakes, and a few of
those fruit cocktail cups that you eat when you're a kid. The kind
with extra cherries.

I want to get far away from Kelby and the beach and my feelings about Kelby and about everything. How far do you have to go
to get away from yourself? I want to go deep into the woods before
I eat. We start out pretty fast, me and the dogs. I'm so used to them
now, I hardly notice their huffing breath and the way they criss-
cross the trail, disappearing and reappearing from the salal. We
go up and west and up and west until I figure that we might be near
the highest peak of the island. My legs are wet from brushing through
the still-rain-soaked undergrowth. There is no lookout provided by
a handy parks department, or signs, or markers, or really anything
at all except a few old trail flags with obscure writing on them, left

here by loggers a decade ago. The trees are thinner up here and there are different kinds than lower down. They are smaller-leaved and spindly. The ground is covered with waist-high yellow grass and thistles and weeds and countless wasps buzzing around on the hard-packed earth. It's hot and somehow the dampness in the air makes it feel like a sauna. I'm soaked in sweat and I miss the bay and the water and I wonder if Kelby is still sitting there and I know that she is.

There are acres of blackberry bushes all around me now. I stuff myself with berries because let's face it, fresh fruit beats tinned sugary stuff anytime. I eat and eat. Thorns scratch patterns in my arms and my hands get sticky with juice. Bees fly around me, brushing against my fingers and legs. I lose track of time. I feel like I'm someone else. Since when am I a kid who picks blackberries on islands? Who am I here?

No one.

By the time I start going down, I've lost my sense of which way I came. But down will eventually lead to a beach and from there, I'll be able to figure out where I am. I pass the face of a cliff off to the side of what must be an old logging road that I'm walking down. I stop. I know that animals live in caves. I know that from movies and books and documentaries.

I know I shouldn't go into the cave.

But knowing a thing and what you do with that knowing are not the same.

I go over to the cave and shout into the entrance. Up close, it's a small space. The entrance is only maybe two feet around. I can't hear anything. I can't smell anything. I remember my dad telling me that all wild animals have an unmistakable stink. A smell you don't have to be an animal to smell. I sniff. I can't smell anything but cool rock and dirt.

I don't know what I'm thinking, but I crawl in. The cave is pretty deep. I crawl about ten feet before I start to feel anxious, but it is so cool that it's a relief from being outside. I lie down on my back.

I don't know why I do that. But I do.

Lying on my back makes me feel buried alive, the roof of the cave only inches above my nose. It's impossible *not* to think about coffins and suddenly I can't breathe, I can't breathe, I can't breathe, but I also can't get out. I mean, to get out, I have to flip back on my belly. I have to wiggle slowly. I have to not panic, but I am panicking, and The King is in the ground in the ground in the ground in the ground.

The King is

The King can't get out

The King is decomposing and

I wiggle out and the dogs sniff me and lick my legs as if to say, *Seriously, dude, don't go into caves.*

"I know," I say to them, scratching each of them behind the ears. "Seriously. What?" I take in huge lungsful of breath.

I try to slow my breathing.

I try to slow my pulse.

It's getting dark.

"Remember the Alamo," I whisper, which is what we always said to each other when we started this game we used to play, this hide-and-seek treasure-hunt game we played in Central Park, but we didn't call it that. We made up a cooler name: SCAT CATS. It's an anagram. Maybe that's only cool if you're a huge nerd, which we are, I guess. *Were*. Whatever.

The point was that you had to find this list of random things, but you couldn't be seen by anyone else. If someone spotted you, you were out. There was a lot of crawling. There was a lot of hiding behind things. A cave like this would have been an awesome find. But nothing is scary when you're with your friends. Everything is scary when you're alone.

Anyway, this one time, one of the things on my list was "wheel," and I thought I'd remembered seeing an old tire down by the edge of this one place on the creek. I don't know why that made sense to me, like I'd be able to carry an old tire back to our meeting place, along with the stuff I already had, which was a balloon on a string, a flamingo, an empty beer bottle, a half-eaten hot dog, and two filthy coins I begged off a street musician, but that's where I was going.

I made my way down the rocky slope that led to this creek. The balloon was basically like a giant red bubble pointing at where I was, so I figured I'd get spotted but there wasn't anything I could do. If I let it go, it would be gone. There was garbage stuck between the rocks and it smelled terrible. I half expected to find a dead body in the water. At least the corpse of a rat. Or worse.

I got down there and the tire I thought I remembered was gone. There was an old shopping cart though and I was trying to figure out how to pull off one of the wheels when I looked up and I saw them.

I saw The King.

He didn't see me. He was talking to someone. A man. He was

with the man. The man and he were together. The man was a middle-aged white guy. Balding. But big, like a biker. He looked somehow tough, even though he was in a suit. I think he was in a suit. Between the man, The King, and me, a woman dressed entirely in long purple robes was doing some kind of tai chi and the purple fabric kept blocking my view.

I don't know why I'm remembering this. I don't know if I'm remembering this right. Probably not.

Or maybe I am.

Suddenly, I'm dizzy. I can't faint in the woods. No one would ever find me and probably a cougar would eat me, so I stop walking and flop down by the trail on a soft patch of moss, in the shade of a huge cedar. I must be getting lower now because the trees are evergreens and ancient. I break off some moss and press the damp roots against my forehead. I don't know why, but ever since I was a kid, when I used to faint, Mom would put a cool cloth on my head and it was like magic, it fixed me. The ground is still damp and a bit muddy from the rain we had last week and the wind is coming up, but I don't really notice that, because I feel like the memory is pushing on me. Crowding me out of myself. I'm remembering something I don't want to remember, I really, really don't want to remember it, I can't *not* remember it, and the dogs are sniffing around my ears and my face like they can figure out what I'm thinking and fix it, that's how it feels, like the dogs always want to fix things and Zeus sits back on his haunches and howls, a full-on howl, which makes me think of sirens, the way the sirens filled the air and drowned out all the other sounds that day while I stared down from the forty-second floor.

So screw me.

I don't know what happened. The King disappeared into the bushes with the man and then came out again, pocketing something.

Money.

He was pocketing money.

He came out of the bushes, pocketing money, and then he ran.

He ran in the opposite direction from where we were meant to meet. He ran like an athlete, not like how he usually ran, he ran so fast and like a freaking Olympic athlete, that I thought maybe it wasn't him after all, knees high, stride long, like there was something he could never run fast enough to get away from.

The man came out right after that. Coughed a few times, in that way people do when they're self-conscious.

I mean, I'm not a total idiot. I know what happened. I know what they did.

I knew it then, too.

I just pretended I didn't.

If I had my phone right now, I'd text Daff. I'd say, *Did you know?* And then she'd say, *Know what?* And I'd say, *About the men in the park.* And she'd say, *Yeah, I knew.* And I'd say, *Why didn't you tell me?* And she'd say, *Because you knew, too.* And then I'd say, *Je suis désolé.* And she'd say, *It sounds better in French*, and then I'd run, I'd puke, I'd run, I'd flip backward off buildings, it would be the ultimate parkour, which maybe, after all, is what he meant for the forty-second floor to be.

And then I'm crying and the dumb dogs are slurping up my tears maybe because they are thirsty or maybe because they aren't so dumb and they are fixing that, too, or maybe I am making them, the way I'm holding on to them too tight and they squirm away from me and sit back on their haunches, staring, like, *What? Dude, enough, let's walk.*

It takes me a long time to start walking again, and the trees are dipping their tops into the darkness like paintbrushes and then swooping the dark low and long in shadows across the trail. I finally come out at a beach but I'm facing the wrong way. I mean, it takes me a while to figure it out, but what I'm looking at isn't Vancouver. I'm on the wrong side. I'm literally miles away from where I am meant to be.

"Crap," I say out loud, and my voice sounds like it's interrupting a conversation the trees were having. I sit down in a little clearing and try to think, how or what or when or where and then I see that what I'm sitting on is a thing, a structure.

It's a grave.

Well, yeah. Of course. I mean, of course. Why not?

People die, you know. People die everywhere. Even on abandoned islands where no one lives, the dead are everywhere.

That's *normal*.

That's just how it is.

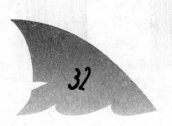

32

THE GRAVES HAVE MOSTLY CRUMBLED OPEN AND THE markers are crooked and some are missing. I look inside one of the collapsed graves. I see bones. I don't want to touch the bones because that seems wrong, but it's like my hand won't stop itself from reaching out, from touching the smooth but dirty round dome of the skull, from resting on the crumbled ribs.

It's a pretty small skeleton. A kid. Or a really small guy, the size of The King. A pile of bones that used to be someone.

I sit back on my haunches and watch the sunset making lazy oranges and yellows spill low across the sky. The water on this side is different, even the beach is different: crushed white shells instead of pebbles. The ground by the beach is a low grassy field instead of stone. It's like being in a different place, at a different time.

I'm cold, from the graveyard or my own cooling sweat. I wish I could light a fire on the beach. The dogs are confused, nervous. "It's okay," I tell them. "It's going to be fine."

The night sky is now full of stars. Because of Kelby, I can

identify the Big Dipper, the Little Dipper, and Cassiopeia. Kelby's on her side of the island, and I'm on mine. I guess she's gone back to her cabin, off the rock. I guess she's safe and warm and probably laughing with Charlie or talking to her mom or playing Monopoly or maybe she's at my cabin, maybe she's wondering where I am. For some reason, I think she's in my room. On my bed. I think she's reading my e-mails. I think she knows about Daff, or she's finding out, and her eyes are widening as she realizes that I'm in love with someone who isn't her, and she knows why I haven't kissed her yet. She must wonder why I haven't kissed her yet. She wants me to kiss her.

Doesn't she?

I wonder if they're worried. I wonder if Dad is freaking out. I wonder if he's thinking about cougars and death.

Eventually, I take my wet towel out of my bag and use it as a blanket. I go to sleep on the white, crunchy shell-sand, above the high-tide line, the dogs pressed against my sides, keeping me warm.

Watching over me.

Protecting me from everything that might come out at night.

33

DAD'S FURIOUS.

"I thought you'd been killed, you idiot. Or that you'd fallen. Do you know how long we looked for you? Do you even care? We even called the RCMP. They were going to come and launch a *search party*. Do you get that? The dogs wouldn't even come when I called. Don't you think I thought the worst? That you'd done some risky climb and tried to flip or whatever you do at the top and missed or . . . worse. *Worse.* I thought maybe you'd—I don't know. *Damn it, kid.* I am so mad. I am so, so mad. I know you don't think of me much as a dad, but I *am* a dad and I didn't deserve that. God, but I am glad you are okay."

"Yeah," I mumble. "Sorry. I was . . . I got turned around. Then it was dark. And, you know, I know there are cliffs and I didn't want to . . . anyway, sorry. I just went the wrong way."

He lurches at me. I think he's going to hit me, so I bring my arms up. "Hey," he says. "Hey," and then he's hugging me. For a second, I feel like burying my face in his shoulder, but then I push him away. I mean, really, too little too late.

"Settle down," I whisper. "I'm fine."

"Don't do that," he says. "Don't ever do that."

"Yeah, yeah," I say. "I'm sorry, okay? I'm sorry."

Then I think about that *srry* on my phone.

Anyway, I don't know why I can't

Sorry is never

"So," I say. "Dad? I'm kind of hungry. Do we have any of those chips?"

He looks at me, frowning. Then he smiles. Then he starts laughing.

Laughter is so weird if you think about it, the way your face scrunches up in spite of what you're feeling, the way your body undulates with the waves of sound that come out of you, even when nothing is funny, and tears pour down your cheeks.

34

HERE IS A THING THAT HAPPENS:

You are sitting on the bench on the point.

The moon is rising over the strait.

The moon is full and kind of red.

Kelby says, "Pumpkin moon. Means someone will be murdered."

You say, "Does not."

She says, "Does too."

You say, "Well, there are only five of us on this whole island, so who is it going to be?"

She says, "Hmm, none of us seems disposable."

You say, "Exactly."

She says, "This is so pretty."

You say, "You are."

She says, "What?"

You say, "You're pretty."

She smiles at you. Behind her, the moon illuminates a long

strip of calm water. A ribbon of moonlight on the road, you think. So you say, "'The highwayman came riding—riding—riding . . . up to the old inn-door.'"

And she says, "I love that poem."

And you lean forward, just slightly, and then you are kissing her and the moon is still behind her but your eyes are closed and she is kissing you back and your hand is on her bare shoulder that has held on to the heat from the afternoon and your hand slides down and she is touching your leg and everything is exactly as it should be and this could go on forever and forever and

"*Gross!*" yells Charlie, from behind you. "I could see your spitty tongue, Kelby."

And, scene.

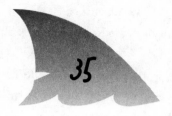

35

I WAKE UP IN THE MORNING AND FEEL GUILTY AND LIKE
I'm in love and like I have to avoid her and like I can't wait to see her
and like I should write to Daff and like I shouldn't ever contact
Daff again and I'm grinning like an idiot.

So yeah, *normal.*

Ish.

Then I feel guilty. Lather, rinse, repeat.

"Good night?" says Dad. Then he continues without waiting
for an answer. "Wanna dive the center today?"

"Huh?" I say.

"Of the strait," he says. "For something different. I know you
guys are getting bored with the reef. Maybe it could be fun."

"Dad," I say. "The reef is never boring." And this is the truest
thing I've ever said. I mean, it's not the Great Barrier Reef, but it's
something.

"It'll be an adventure," he says. "Hey, maybe something will happen and I can write about it, because I've gotta admit, this book is sagging in the middle."

"Right," I say. "Okay. Adventure."

But what I'm thinking is Kelby, Kelby, Kelby.

Which isn't good.

The thing with girls is that you shouldn't let them get to you. You shouldn't let them get in. Because next thing you know, they're under your skin, like scabies. An itch you can't scratch.

Not that Kelby is scabies.

Not that Daff is scabies.

Nah, girls aren't *scabies*. Girls are—

Dad interrupts. "Let's move it, son, while the water is calm as a baby's butt."

"Okay, okay," I say. I dump my dish in the sink and grab my stuff from the hook. "Ready, old man?" I say.

"Yeah, yeah," he says. "I'm coming." He gathers up his camera and his gear and food and drinks and, weighed down, we make our way to the boat in the bay.

Kelby always goes first, sits on the edge of the boat, waiting for the right moment. The problem is that she won't make eye contact. The whole way out here, her eyes drifted off me, like they couldn't stick if they tried. Her hands tap out songs on her leg.

I think she mouths something to me right before she puts her mouthpiece back in and disappears, but I don't catch it. I feel a shiver of something that might be dread but I can't figure out what's wrong. Charlie is eagerly snapping photos with Dad's camera, like our own personal National Geographic paparazzi. Darcy is at the wheel. Kelby drops into the sea.

Then it's my turn.

The water this deep is a different color, more blue-gray than green, or maybe that's because it's cloudy out today, the sun veiled with the haze of coming rain. Without the reef there to show where we are, it's super disorienting, like we're diving into outer space. There are no edges. It takes me a few minutes to adjust to the openness, to find Kelby, to follow her flippers as she descends into the darkness.

It does look dark.

It's not really so very deep, so it seems wrong how fast the light filters away.

How soon we're in the dusky low light of deep water.

Anxiety prickles at my neck. The dives we did before were so shallow you could see the seafloor from the boat when the water was clear. This is something altogether different. This feels too real. It feels bigger than me. Like how kissing Kelby felt. Like I was letting go of something or falling into something that could eat me alive.

I try to keep my breathing calm and under control, but it's hard not to take fast breaths. I start thinking about this guy I heard about on a podcast who was cave diving somewhere in Southeast Asia. It was so dark you couldn't see where you were or where you were going, and I guess he got tangled in the safety rope at the bottom and died, and then this other guy went in to get the body, and he died, too. I'm not telling the story well because trust me when I say it was the most terrifying thing I've ever heard.

I shouldn't be thinking about stuff that's scary, I should be thinking how lucky I am, how this is beautiful, but all I can see are

Kelby's green flippers and the water is murky, which I know is silt from the river across the strait, but it's disconcerting and ugly.

I want it to be over.

It takes ages to get to the bottom. I don't know how deep we are, but the surface looks a lifetime away. I check my tanks because I feel like I've already used all my air. I'm light-headed. The gauge says I'm fine, but I don't feel fine. I point up and Kelby shakes her head no, we just got here. She looks puzzled. I shrug, point at my gauge. She swims over and looks and makes a gesture of, *What? It's fine!* I slow my breathing. Nod.

Okay. Fine.

There is much less to see here than at the reef. The seafloor is flatter than I would have expected, littered with rocks and a few waterlogged logs and some low-lying gray-looking grassy weed. We are too far away from the light. I point up again. I don't like the way the ocean feels open behind me and in front. I don't like the way I can't see an edge.

She looks around, makes a gesture I don't understand. Then she starts to rise, following her bubbles. I wait until she is a few feet above me, and then I start to follow.

Which is when I see it.

I'm sure I see it.

Look, this will sound

I know what I saw

I know what I see

It might be hard to

About twenty feet away, moving fast through the water is a white.

A great white.

It's the biggest shark I've ever seen.

I can't reach Kelby's foot to get her attention. My brain unravels. Everything I love about sharks dissolves into a montage from *Jaws*.

Suddenly, he's so close I could touch him. He's curious, I tell myself. Not hungry. Not on the attack. But I stop breathing. I swallow wrong. My throat closes and I'm choking. How has she not looked back? How can she not see this? Some buddy.

The shark flicks his tail in slow-motion—the water he moves pushes against my face—and he disappears into the shadows to my left.

I know she didn't see it. She's so far away. She didn't wait.

When I get to the surface, she's already on the boat. My heart is practically pounding out of my chest.

". . . sort of boring," she is saying. "Not much down there. Not like I imagined—oh, there you are. What happened to you? You're supposed to stay close." She sounds mad.

"There was a . . . ," I say. "Sorry? I—" I'm gulping air like a thirsty guy in a desert. "Sorry, I'm—"

"What's with you?" she says. "You know you can't swim off and do your own thing."

"There was a shark," I whisper. It comes out thin and unsubstantial. A ghost of what I wanted to say.

"Whatever," she says. She mumbles under her breath, "Douchebag."

"What?" I say. "Seriously. There was a shark."

"Maybe we should not talk," she says. "Sharkboy." Her voice is heavy with sarcasm and I realize she's never called me that before.

"There was a freaking huge shark," I say.

"I'm sure," she says. "That only you could see. Was there also a unicorn?"

"Are you guys fighting?" says Charlie. "Are you mad?"

"No," I say, at the same time as she is saying, "Yes."

No one talks on the way in, like my muteness is contagious. Like I've sucked all the joy out of these people and this place.

The waves are coming up and the boat hits the chop hard and we wouldn't be able to hear each other anyway. It starts to rain, gently at first and then harder and then it's a downpour.

I can't stop thinking about the shark. It was there. I know it was. Wasn't it?

The shape of it in the water, like a shadow, but present. Solid. Real. The way the weight of the water was pushed toward me when he left, a force of nature. But did it, after all, seem as real as the whales? The whales made sounds, clicking and whistling. Sharks are silent. Was that the difference? Or was the shark only an idea I wanted to see? Like Kelby's ghosts. So am I crazy? Did I make it up? Was it really there? Does it matter if we see a thing or if we just think we see a thing? And what's the difference?

Dad wouldn't believe me. Charlie would probably be scared. Darcy would . . . I don't know. Pray? And Kelby? Well, she thinks I'm lying. And now, apparently, we're fighting and I haven't even got the first idea why.

There are so rarely whites in these waters. It hardly ever happens.

It probably didn't happen at all.

But when I get back to the cabin, I climb up to my bed and I pick up my broken phone and plug it in. When I slide my hand over the screen, the edges of the glass are sharp against my fingers. I text Daff, *I saw a great white shark.* The sentence feels flimsy to me. Surreal. I can't think of what I can add or take away to give it the weight that it needs. An exclamation mark? A paragraph of description?

I saw a great white shark.

There is a shark here.

J'ai vu un grand blanc.

Un grand blanc est ici maintenant.

Why don't I know the word for shark in French?

I pick a phrase and this time I hit Send and even though the screen is broken, somehow the pigeons manage to lift the message away and then *swoooop*, they are gone, on their way to New York, on their way to a different world, with my message that doesn't mean anything to anyone but me. My finger makes a tiny bloody fingerprint on the Send icon on the screen, so small that you'd never notice it unless you were looking, one tiny drop of crimson on an expanse of broken glass.

36

"I DON'T KNOW," SHE SAYS, LATER, ON THE DECK, A BOTTLE of beer in front of her covered with flecks of rain. "The cards are wet. I can't shuffle these."

"I don't want to play cards," I say. Inside the cabin, the circle of light from the candles illuminates Dad and Darcy and Charlie playing Monopoly. "I want to talk about how you can, you know, kiss me like that and then be completely hostile to me the next day."

"Yeah," she says. "That's why I said 'I don't know.' Don't you ever just not know?"

"I know I like kissing you," I say. "Nothing has to be a big deal unless you make it a big deal."

"You're an idiot," she says. "Kissing is always a big deal. Tell Mum I went home to read, 'kay?" She drops the cards on the table where they land in the pooling rain puddle. Water drips off my hair and into my eyes.

I don't say anything.

I sit in the rain.

I watch her go.

Eventually, I get up and go down to the bay and climb up onto the rock. The night has submerged itself into the black water, sliding into it like the seals do when they are startled off the reef, spilling over into it, so the blackness of it is everywhere. I sit on the wet rock, which sticks to the back of my legs, and I try not to think about anything I don't want to think about. I lie down on my back and stare up at the sky until the clouds thin and start to part and I can see stars freckling through. After a while, the tide starts to rise and the moon starts to glow through the veil of black wisps. I toss stones into the water and see the stars reflected there, except it isn't the stars, it's phosphorescence in the water itself and it's so gorgeous and I yell, *"Kelby!"* And I know she can hear me because you can hear everything here, but she doesn't come, so I strip down to my shorts and I swim, my hands picking up handfuls of stars, the light pouring off my skin in trailing drops.

31

IN THE COURTYARD OF THE UNBUILT HOTEL, THERE IS A patch of rock, twenty feet by twenty feet. It is almost entirely flat, except for a crack about three feet from one edge that runs the length of the square. We have our drinks stuck in the crack and a sleeping bag spread out that we are lying on. Charlie keeps getting up, finding things like caterpillars and termites, leaves and sticks. "Look at this!" he'll say, excited. "Look at this!"

I look every time. I mean, he's a nice kid.

"There," Kelby says, pointing up.

"That's so ridiculous," I tell her. "You're pointing at the sky. That could be anywhere in the sky!"

"Follow my finger," she says.

"Come on," I say. "You're pointing at every star. It's impossible to tell which one you mean."

"I see it, I see it," chants Charlie, without looking up. "I see the stars."

"Fine," she says. "It's sort of like a *Y*. Can you see the *Y*?"

I look at the stars. I can't see a Y. I see a million dots of light. A billion. An infinite number of stars shaken out like salt across the universe. I don't tell Kelby that looking at stars makes me feel anxious because I know that looking at stars makes her feel safe.

A satellite spins its way from east to west, the spin making it appear to flash on and off.

"I used to think they were UFOs," she says. "I used to hope they'd come and get me."

"Will they?" says Charlie, finally looking up. "Cool."

"No," she says.

"Why?" I said. "What's so terrible about your life that being, like, I don't know, *probed*, would be better? What if they performed experiments on you? What if they put ball bearings in your ears or something and you didn't discover it until you went through airport security? What if they implanted you with an alien baby? Then what?"

"You watch too much TV," she says. "That's crazy. Besides, I was a kid. It just seemed like it would be a good adventure. To go somewhere else, you know? To be someone else."

I nudge her with my arm. "You're okay, just as you are," I say. I'm sort of flirting, sort of not, mostly because I'm kind of scared of her and I don't know if she wants me to flirt or not. I don't know if I want to or not. Because *Daff*. In the moonlight, Kelby's hair looks silver, her profile looks like something you would find etched on an ancient coin.

"Yeah," she says. "I'm not so great. You only think so because you don't know me."

"Really?" I say. "What don't I know? What terrible thing would make me not like you?"

"She's sort of mean sometimes," says Charlie.

"I like mean people," I say.

Kelby sighs and closes her eyes for a brief moment. It's so quiet here that her sigh is the loudest sound and then there's the rustle of the sleeping bag as she pulls her knees up.

"Shooting star!" I say, watching one scream past the satellite and vanish.

She opens her eyes.

"Hey," she says. "I was reading this thing about what would happen if a meteor hit the earth again. Like a big one, I mean. Like the one that wiped out the dinosaurs. It said that if it was really big, we wouldn't know it was coming until it was too late. Like an astronomer somewhere would see it and before he'd even be able to finish the thought, *I see a meteor*, it would have hit and it would basically just vaporize everything and everyone within a certain number of miles. Vaporize them. They wouldn't even know it was happening or had happened. They'd be at Costco, buying a life-time supply of dill pickles, and then they'd just see a bright light and then they'd *be* the bright light. You know?"

"Wow," I say. "Dill pickles?"

"Seriously," she says. "That's what you got out of that? Dill pickles?"

She sounds mad, so I say, "Kidding! That's terrible. I mean, terrifying." I stare up at the dusty-light stars and think about it. It is kind of terrifying, actually. To think that at any second that could happen. Now. Or *now*. Or . . . now.

"I think it's sort of beautiful," she says. "Like poetry. Becoming the light. But not being able to prepare for it. I think people waste all this time preparing for things. Planning them. But we aren't in charge. Are the pickles important? Maybe every minute of your life should be spent doing something that's important enough that if the light comes for you, you know that you're going out doing something that matters. Not that you'd have time to think that over, I guess."

"What do you mean?" I say.

"Well, you're dead," she says. "And then your brain shuts down and whatever you think you see is just your brain sending this frantic kind of last dream to you on your way out. Plus a bunch of euphoria, I guess. Then you're gone."

"Hang on," I say. "What? I mean, that doesn't sound like the words of someone who believes in ghosts. How does *that* work?"

"I don't know," she says. "I don't really know anything. No one does. We just pretend to know stuff and say it like we mean it and people believe us. If you say things people want to hear, they believe you more."

"Uh-oh," says Charlie. "I've gotta pee." He takes off running down the path.

"Charlie!" she yells. *"Be careful!"*

"I'm always careful!" he shouts. Then, "Ouch." Then, "I'm okay! *Bye!"*

She laughs, and so do I. I guess maybe this is the perfect moment to kiss her again, but I don't.

I can't.

And I don't know why not.

38

THE NEXT DAY IS A SUNDAY AFTERNOON OR IT MIGHT
be a Monday, it doesn't matter here. I go up to the hotel early to work
out, running slowly around the entire perimeter of the top wall of
the structure, jumping the small gaps, like doing laps. I don't look
down because when I do I'm rocked by waves of vertigo, rolling me
back and forth, sideways on my feet. I look only at the beam and
my feet, which are bare and blackened from the trail up, thickened
from a summer of rocks and barnacles and the earth.

I do about ten laps, sweat pouring off me, before I see him.

Charlie.

He's kneeling in the courtyard, slowly spinning to keep me in his
line of vision. I pretend I don't see him and do another lap, a sort of
show-offy lap with a couple of things where I drop down and swing
from my arms onto the lower beam. I know he thinks I'm basically
the coolest person on earth and hey, not many people feel that way.

Finally, I come down. I come up behind him, where he is

examining a trail of termites that are marching across the rock in a line, like ants, intent on getting to their next meal.

"They grow wings, you know," he says. "Like at the end of the summer, they all just get these wings at once and take off and they are really bad at flying, so they get in your hair. It's pretty cool."

"Wow," I say. "Really? I didn't know."

"Yeah," he says. "Kelby gets totally freaked out. Because one flew in her mouth once."

"Gross," I say.

"Yeah," he says. Then he starts laughing in his Charlie way, his laugh taking over his whole body, shaking him all the way down to his carefully tied shoes. "In her mouth." He gasps, tears streaming down his face.

I smile to let him know that it's all right to laugh, but it's not that funny.

Finally, he goes, "Can you teach me?"

And I'm like, "Teach you what?" My eyes sting from the sweat dripping in them and I'm dying to go back to the cabin for a cold drink, maybe lie in the shade for a while. Read a book.

"That," he says, pointing up.

"No way," I tell him. "That's not for kids. You have to be big. Like me."

He stops laughing. He stops smiling. His broken tooth disappears under his lip. "Oh yeah," he says. "Okay. Forget it." Then, before I can tell he's going to cry, he starts to run away.

"Hey!" I say, running after him. "Wait up!"

"Go away!" he yells, running faster, tripping over the massive root of a maple tree that sprawls lazily across the path, pushing up the earth and rocks in its way. "Leave me alone!"

"I'm sorry," I call. "Come back. I'll teach you something. Please? Charlie?"

But he's gone, vanished into the thick salal path that leads down to their place. I follow him a good distance behind until I make sure that I see him on his own deck, panting hard from the exertion, shrugging off his mom's hug. Then I go back up to the nameless hotel and lie down in the central square. It's kind of sad that it was never named anything. I wonder what they thought it was going to be. I wonder what they imagined. Not this, that's for sure. No one could possibly have pictured this skeleton of a building, unfinished, exposed, rotting in the elements. The rock under my back is doing nothing to cool me off. Up in the sky, white puffy clouds move by too quickly. The wind must be coming up. I close my eyes for a second, a minute, but the minute turns into an hour, and I dream of The King, of the day when I said, casually, "Hey, can you teach me that stuff?" and how he laughed at me and said, "You idiot, you just *do* it. There's nothing to know." And how I tried running up the wall, and fell, hard, back on my head, but in my dream, that's not how it goes, instead the movie reel jerks to halt there, and then instead of falling, I keep running and running and I'm running up the side of a skyscraper made from mirrored glass, except that I'm so close to it I can see the silhouettes of office workers in cubicles, sipping coffee, staring at screens, and I run faster and faster up the wall, the sky at the wrong angle to me and my feet hitting the glass hard enough to crack it and then, at the top, I push off, and I tuck my head to my chest, ready to flip back down to the ground, and then I'm falling and falling and falling and yeah, of course, I wake up, you always do before you hit the ground, right?

My face is sunburned and my body hurts and that sort of feels right. I go back to the cabin, where Dad is hunched over his type-writer, punching the keys hard, and he says, "Got a minute? Could you read this chapter for me?"

I guess because I hate myself and everything already hurts, I nod, and he hands me this sheaf of paper and I take it to the ham-mock to read in the shade of the old-growth cedar, to the sound of the tide slowly moving in the pass in front of me.

39

Dear Daff,

It's been a while since I wrote to you. You've stopped texting me or it's stopped working, which is good. You should *stop texting me*. You should stop. This *should stop*.

I mean, I thought you'd answer because of the shark.

But the more I think about it, the more I think it wasn't real. My brain was telling me what it thought I wanted to hear. People do that. Brains do that.

I kissed Kelby and now she's

I kissed Kelby

I think I like Kelby

I don't think I like Kelby

I don't know what I mean anymore about anything. Maybe it's only a trick of the light: the shark, my feelings for Kelby, the kiss, the way I miss you.

Remember The King's birthday party last year with the magician and that black light? We were all glowing white *shirts and teeth and shadows and he cut you in half, the magician, and there were your feet and there was your head and that was so weird. I still don't get it. I know it's mirrors. But I don't know how they work. So you can know you're being tricked and still not understand why, I guess is the thing. I remember The King was seeing that girl from St. X. I can't remember her name but she was super hot and then in the black light, there was that dusting of white on her shoulder and afterward he said he couldn't date a girl who didn't notice that she had dandruff and we never saw her again. I think he was a pretty unforgiving guy. You know, sometimes I try really hard to think about the stuff I liked about him, and it's like it's slipping away. Like there must have been something, but I can't grab hold of it, and then I'm worried that he was right all along, that I liked him because he was rich and sort of famous or maybe, I don't know, I grabbed at the first lifeboat from the sinking ship and never really thought about it. You don't, right? You don't spend a lot of time thinking, "Gee, why is this person my friend?" You just are friends. Half the time they drive you crazy, and the other half they feel like an extension of you, your arm or your foot, and you kind of take that for granted and then they die and you have this terrible phantom pain where they were before they went.*

Maybe it's like that.

I have to really think about what you looked like, Daff. These two months have been forever.

You know how sometimes enough stuff happens that you

start to feel like your entire life up until a certain point was a dream and the only thing that is real is what happens after that? So if everything was a dream until The King died, then everything that is real is about me getting away from you and stopping loving you, so I was just lying in the hammock, reading my dad's incredibly terrible book, which, by the way, is called The Hotel Neverwas—*which is so weird because I'd just been thinking about how it's kind of sad that half-built hotel never got a name. My dad and I think alike, I guess. I think it's about what he imagines I'm doing here and instead is just a really confusing story about a teenage boy who probably thinks and acts a lot more like a normal teenage boy than I do. I feel like when I'm reading it, I'm reading how a normal person would act. Like, look! An otter! Cool! I can steal a beer from my dad! Party! A pretty girl! Whooo-hoo!*

Which maybe is how I think, after all.

Anyway, the book made me so mad that I "accidentally" let a couple of pages blow away.

I don't know why I did that.

It's just this thing between Dad and me, where just when I feel like we can really see each other, he shows me that I'm wrong.

I know it's his only copy, because he types on an actual typewriter, like he thinks he's Hemingway with his beard and his island retreat. I wonder if Hemingway would wear ironic T-shirts if he was still alive. I bet he would. I bet the hilarity of the ironic T-shirt would keep him from killing himself and he'd be alive and writing scripts for Marvel comics remakes for Paramount or something. Everyone is such a phony if you think about it. He'd probably sell out, too.

Not that Dad has sold out. The thing is that no one is buying what Dad is selling.

Darcy went over to the mainland for supplies and she bought us a bunch of stuff, like ice cream and cereal and milk and cheese and steaks and fresh vegetables and fruit and somehow in one of our bags, there was a magazine, a stupid magazine, and on the front cover there was a tiny picture of you.

You, Daffodil Blue.

Can you even?

I mean, what the——? How did this happen?

Now I am so angry at you. I am so mad, Daff. I am punch-the-wall mad. I want my fist to hurt. I want my skin to crack open so I can hate you even more for hurting my hand because I'm so mad, but I'm not doing that. I'm not going to.

I guess The King falling off that building was the best thing that happened to you and now you're going to be in a movie—a movie—and what? I mean, seriously, what? Who ARE you? And I guess you can see why all of this seems like the nightmare that comes after the dream that I had up until The King died.

The King died.

The King died.

The King died.

The other day I was out rowing this little wooden dinghy that Dad has. I rowed as far out into the Salish Sea as I dared. I mean, you really wouldn't want to be in that little half-rotted thing when the waves came up, that's the truth. I rowed all the way out there and then I lay down in the hull and felt the waves slapping against the keel, and imagined that shark down there beneath me, the imaginary shark that I dreamed up, the one I wanted to see, I guess. And while the boat rocked, this seagull landed on the bow. He wasn't looking at me, he was looking out toward Vancouver, and he just started calling in this really rhythmic chant and it sounded just like that to me, "The King died, The King died, The King died."

Then he crapped, narrowly missing my face by a few inches, and flew off.

Which has got to be a metaphor for something, right?

I don't know what you're doing right now or if you're even in New York, or if you're in LA and getting an agent and befriending starlets or rock stars or whatever the next steps are for you in becoming famous and being someone else.

You know, just this second, as I typed that, I forgave you. Weird, right?

Forgive is a word that's made of tissue paper and folded into a flower and just as you hand it to the other person it bursts into flame and singes their skin. That's what it looks like to me, anyway.

Enjoy the movies! I have someone else I have to hand a rose to, too. Two, too, to.

I wish I could see you. Remember the Alamo.

Love,

JC

40

"LOOK," KELBY SAYS. "PRETEND WE NEVER KISSED AND GET over it. You are the worst. You make such a big deal about everything! It isn't a big deal. We kissed, it was dumb, we are moving on. So. It's not a big deal, you want to dive today or not? We're going to dive the pass because the current is so small today. There are, like, octopuses. Octopi. Whatever. And it's nice out. So whatever, come. Don't come. I don't care."

"Wow," I say. "That's quite the invitation." I grin. It's hard to pretend I'm not glad to see her. "Yes."

"Great," she says. "Get your stuff and I'll meet you in an hour, okay?"

"Okay," I say.

I go into the cabin to find Dad, to give him back his chapter.

He practically leaps out of his chair, tripping over the dogs, who are taking their afternoon nap on the cool tile floor of the living room. "So?" he says. "Whadja think?"

"Yeah," I lie. "Really good, Dad. Wow. Totally the next Harry Potter."

"You think?" he says. "But it's not paranormal. Paranormal is so hot right now. Maybe I could make it paranormal."

"Yeah, Dad," I say. I can't believe he's buying it. "You could do that, but this is already fine. Fantastic. Really great."

"I am so relieved," he said. "I thought maybe it was garbage and I was wasting my life!" He laughs a little too hard. I think about those two pieces of paper, the typing squashed together, single-spaced, and how they blew into the pass, and landed on the surface, the water slowly seeping into the paper and ink, swirling it into nothing, the tide pools sucking them down into the murk. Maybe I'll find them today. Maybe an octopus will be reading them thoughtfully, slowly nodding his approval at Dad's massive overuse of adverbs. SUDDENLY, HE THOUGHTFULLY TAPPED HIS PEN TO HIS DEEPLY WRINKLED BROW.

"Dad," I say.

But he looks so stupidly happy and I am such a jerk.

"Yeah?" he says.

"I'm going out," I tell him. "We're going to see the octopuses."

"Great," he says happily. "They are seriously amazing. You know, we have the biggest ones in the world here? Wave to me! I'll be right here. I'm so fired up now, I may even finish the next chapter for you to read when you get back. Steak tonight?"

"Sure, Dad," I say. "We'll check the traps for prawns."

We drop these prawn traps down every time we go out and then pull them up the next time. Last time, they were empty—someone else must have gotten there first—but maybe today they'll be full. Mrs. S. would be so proud of me, I think. Mrs. S. would love these prawns and scallops. She'd hold the fan shell of the scallop up to her cheek and she'd coo like she was talking to a baby, *So beautiful*, she'd say. *So miraculous, no? And so expensive! Florida, here we come!* Then she'd give me some for free.

I don't know if Mrs. S. will ever get to Florida. She gives too much away.

And suddenly, I'm rooted to the spot, tears in my eyes, thinking about those free shrimp. I clear my throat. "Yeah, we'll get some prawns today, I bet." Then, "Dad, have you talked to Mom? It's been a while since I've heard anything."

He looks surprised. "No," he says. "I never talk to her. She hasn't texted?"

"I—" I say. "Um, I sort of broke my phone. I might have missed—anyway, I'll send her an e-mail later. It's no big deal."

Dad nods, his glasses sliding down his nose, his fingers tapping the table like he's already typing the next chapter in his head. He's got all the crazy of a real writer, but none of the skill. That cringing feeling that I get sometimes when I look at him washes over me. "Dad," I say. "I'm—I'll see you later, okay?"

I whistle for the dogs and grab the diving stuff and make my way down to the beach to wait for Kelby. On my way, I see Charlie at his usual position at the tide pool. "Hey," I say. "Are you coming diving?"

He shakes his head, won't look at me.

"I'll teach you," I tell him. "Come on, don't be mad."

He still won't look at me. I crouch down next to him and nudge him with my arm.

"Pleeeeease forgive me?" I say. "C'mon, buddy. There are basically no people on the island except for us and you guys, and if you're mad at me, it's effectively like 25 percent of the population hates me. I can't take it!" I grab my chest in mock horror and roll back onto the sandstone rock. "Nooooo!"

Then suddenly he's grinning. "After dinner?" he says. "After dinner. Right? Right? Okay?"

And I go, "Yeah, okay. You coming on the boat?"

And Charlie says, "Yeah, I'm coming, dummy. 'Course I'm coming. I'm always on the boat. I'm in charge of the flag, remember? Duh."

Together we run down the path, the three panting dogs, the kid, and me, the sun beating down on the trees throwing cool shade on us, protecting us from the afternoon heat, our feet slipping on the arbutus leaves that are starting to drop onto the path, signaling that summer is thinking about coming to a close before I'm really ready for fall.

41

WE COME UP FROM THE DIVE WITHOUT HAVING SEEN AN
octopus. Not that it matters. The sea was so clear today it was like
floating in air, crystal clear. Jellyfish moved by on the current and a
large school of herring darted around us. On the surface, we could
see birds diving for the fish, their beaks puncturing the protective
bubble of the surface water, hungry mouths grabbing for more.

I've got to be honest, I felt lucky. Lucky to be on this weird
island, lucky to be in this sea, lucky to be seeing the stuff I was
seeing.

I didn't even realize I was thinking about sharks, but I was,
because I was thinking about how perfectly it works, with the fish
and the birds, the exchange of life for life, which made me think of
death, which made me think of The King and made me wonder,
What was the trade? What did the world get out of the deal? Space
for one more person? It was the first time I thought about The King
without feeling nauseated, so that was progress, but maybe that's
because I had my mouthpiece in and was breathing through my

mouth. Through the long stems of kelp, I could see a few rock cod lying on the seafloor, almost perfectly disguised. A dogfish darted by. It was so freaking magical and alive and perfect, that's all I was thinking.

I think I was just happy.

Plain old happy.

Like I was before, pretty often, hanging with The King and Daff, doing the crazy stuff we did, there were lots of times I felt like that, like I was a part of everything. I was where I was meant to be.

So when Kelby signals that it's time to go up, I rise slowly to the surface, not wanting this to end. The last flicker of the silver fish vanishing beyond the point where I can see them, the sun at first too bright, the boat bobbing a short distance away. By the time I get my mask off though, I know something is wrong because Darcy looks worried and Charlie is trying so hard to say something that nothing is coming out of his mouth.

I climb up the ladder onto the boat and say, "Whoa, kid, what?"

And Kelby is saying, "What happened? What happened?"

And Darcy is shaking her head.

And Charlie is stuttering, "Sh-sh-sh-shark."

And Darcy guns the engine and roars in to shore.

42

NO ONE WANTS TO HEAR ABOUT HOW SHARKS ARE
really unlikely to bite a person. No one seems to care that shark
bites are pretty much unheard of in the Pacific Northwest. No one
cares about any of what I'm saying about protecting the sharks and
balance in the oceans and the oxygen and the plankton and the
food chain. It's like a horror movie of hysterical reactions, which I
guess is predictable but also totally disappointing.

Dad is going crazy. "You could have been killed! You could
have been killed! You could have died! Don't you get it? You'd be
dead. Even if he'd just taken a bite, you would have bled out.
There's no hospital here. You'd be dead. Dead."

Stop, I want to tell him. *Stop*. But he keeps saying it, that word,
dead, over and over again and I can't breathe and my voice is leaking out of me and I can't do this and I can't listen to this and what
is he proposing anyway, it's a shark that's out of its migratory path,
for sure, but it isn't interested in us when there are so many seals,

it has probably already had a meal that may feed it for weeks or even months, it can't be hungry with all this life and stop. *Stop.*

"*No,*" I manage. "It's not *Jaws,* Dad. It's not going to—"

"What if it bit Charlie? Or Kelby? Or Darcy? We have to call someone. We have to tell someone. What do they do in these cases? What do they do? Is there a 'they'?"

His eyes are wild and he's basically freaking out, so I say, "God, Dad, the water is full of sharks and none have ever eaten Charlie or Kelby or Darcy or anyone else except in really rare cases and—"

"THIS IS NOT A DOCUMENTARY FILM!" he yells. "YOU ARE NOT ROB WHAT'S-HIS-NAME! THIS IS NOT A GOD-DAMN MOVIE!" Apollo yelps and disappears under the deck of the cabin, which is where he goes to escape drama and the sun. Zeus follows, looking depressed. He casts a glance back at me. I shrug. "I'd run, too," I whisper.

"DAD," I yell back. "YOU ARE SCARING THE DOGS!"

"YOU ARE!" he yells. "GODDAMNIT, SHARKY."

"Hey," I say. "I'm not the bad guy here! I'm—"

"You're not . . . ," he says. "You're not a *shark.*"

"Dad," I say. "I know. But it is only passing through. It's just off course. It's not eating people. You would have heard if it was. There are a million seals! If it's hungry, which I doubt, it will eat a seal. It probably already has. It won't eat again now for ages."

"No one goes in the water," he says. "Until I've talked to some-one. Until I know what to do."

"But I am someone," I say. "And I've told you. He's not going to bite anyone. He's probably already a hundred miles away. Are you just never going in the water again? I mean, I saw him a while ago and no one—"

"WHAT?" he yells. "What? You SAW him? You SAW him and you went back in the water? You let Charlie back in the water? Kelby? Darcy? ME? You SAW THE SHARK AND YOU DIDN'T MENTION IT?"

"Dad," I say. "I wasn't sure. I wasn't sure what I saw. I thought maybe I was imagining . . . and . . . I don't know. I thought it was kind of like a sign, maybe. I thought it was like a sign for me. From The King. I'm sure that sounds stupid to you—"

"JESUS," he swears. "Not everything is about your friend killing himself! NOT EVERYTHING IS ABOUT YOU. You put other people at risk! You . . . idiot. You're an idiot. I don't even know . . ."

But I don't hear the rest, because I'm off and running, my feet hardly hitting the ground, and I'm going so fast that I'm outrunning the shadows, it's only me and the sun blurring into one beam of white-hot light, running with all the rage and pain and hurt churning around inside me like chum on the surface of the sea, calling the shark to slaughter.

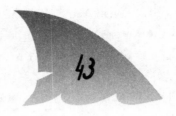

43

DAD AND DARCY ARE SITTING ON THE FRONT PORCH
couch when I get back, spent and sweaty. I can hear the conversation before they can see me.

"Without a picture, they don't believe me anyway," Dad is saying. "They think I'd make it up! Can you imagine? Like I mistook a mud shark for a dangerous shark or something?"

"But he's probably right," Darcy says. "It's probably long gone. Anyway, I agree with him that nothing would happen. God has us covered. He knows that we . . ."

". . . that he didn't tell us sooner," says Dad. "Putting our *lives* at risk."

I stomp heavily up the steps and their conversation slams to a stop as effectively as if I ran a train into it.

"Where's Charlie?" I say. "I told him I'd teach him parkour."

"What?" says Darcy. "I think he's too young for that."

I shrug. "He doesn't think so. I'm not going to let him fall off a building or anything. I'm only going to teach him the first things you have to know, like jumping high in place. That kind of thing. So he can jump over stuff. It's no big deal, but if you don't want me to—"

"I didn't say that," says Darcy. "Just be careful, okay? He kind of worships you, you know."

"Yeah, right," I say. "I'm sure. Anyway, where is he?"

"Tide pool," calls Kelby. She's in the hammock. I didn't see her before because she's so small and it's folded so that she's basically been swallowed by it.

"Hey," I say. "Are you coming?"

"Yeah," she says. "I guess. More interesting than lying here listening to these two plot to kill a shark that's as big as the boat. I'm just mad we didn't see it. We must have been looking at the herring."

"Yep," I say, heading down toward the tide pool. "I guess we were."

"Sometimes you have to really look to see a thing," she says. "I know *that* feeling."

"Kelby," I say. "What's your book about? Can I read it?"

She stops in her tracks. She looks at me carefully, up and down, like she's measuring me up. Then a flash of teeth, and she's smiling.

"Okay," she says. "Whatever. Maybe. *Charlie! Let's go!*"

Charlie comes darting up the steps toward us, like he'd been hanging there the whole time, waiting for us to show up.

"Hey!" he says, trying to sound cool. "Is it time? Is it time now? Wasn't that shark cool? What did you think, Sharky? Because, like, did you even think that you'd see anything like that here? Did you?

Did you? I mean, Mum is *freaking out!* But that's dumb, right? Sharks don't bite people, you said. Not much, anyway. Sharky? Are we going? Now?"

Kelby laughs. "Slow down, sport. Take a breath."

"I *am* breathing!" he says. "Am I breathing right for parkour, Sharky? Am I?"

"You know what?" I say. "Call me JC."

"Okay," he says. "JC. Can we go? Now?"

I whistle for the dogs and they come running and we head up to Hotel Neverwas for the first lesson. It's the first part that's the hardest. That's the part where you learn how to jump. How high you can go. Where you have to trust that even though it seems impossible, if you believe you can fly, then you really can.

Not far. Not from the forty-second floor. But far enough to get from this log to that one. Far enough to clear the beam.

Charlie is a good student. He jumps and jumps and jumps and jumps, over and over again. Never giving up, not even when his skinned knees are bleeding and his arms are bruised. I remember being like that, I guess. I just don't know if I still am, or if that part of me jumped off the building at the same time as The King did. Maybe it was never me, after all. Maybe it was just him, reflecting on me.

Anyway, I teach Charlie how to jump. That's always the first thing. And I guess I do it the right way, because on the way back down the path, Kelby's hand finds mine and holds on tight. I try not to squeeze it. It feels like a bird, resting there, just waiting to take flight.

44

I'M RUNNING.

It feels good. Hot, sweaty, hard work. The rocks are on such an angle that it makes it harder, which feels right.

I'm about a mile down the beach from the cabin when I run out of steam. My legs are cramping up and I'm thirsty but I didn't bring a drink.

I take off my shoes and socks and stick my feet in a tide pool. An anemone opens and closes near my big toe. A small fish tickles my ankles before darting for safety under a crack. I try to simply *be*. It's really quiet. I lie back on the warmed stone and stare up at the sky. At the edge of my view are the tops of the trees, leaning out of the forest for a better view of the sea. The tide is low, so rocks encrusted with bladder wrack—this brownish seaweed that is covered with "popping balloons" as Charlie calls them—are basking in the sun. Out on the reef, there is a distinct absence of seals, but I can see an otter fishing in the small shell-sand bay about a hundred feet south of me. Behind me, up a yellow grassy hill, an

A-frame cabin sits empty and unfinished, like the owner ran out of energy for completing it, returned to Vancouver or wherever he was from, and didn't look back. I can hear grasshoppers on the hill. The call of gulls diving into the water, probably still looking for herring for lunch. Kingfishers screech at each other and skim low over the surface of the water. At the tide line, a heron stands on one foot, stock-still, staring out to sea.

And suddenly, I miss Daff.

I miss her with an ache that cramps my guts.

"Daff," I say out loud.

I mean, it's one thing to be here, but then, if you start thinking about it, it's also like you're trapped here.

I sit up and stare at the calm sea, willing a dorsal fin to appear. Waiting for something to happen.

From a long way away, I can hear the whine of boat engines. When it's calm like this, sounds travel like crazy across the water, magnified. The whine comes closer. I look in the direction of the sound, not for any reason, but because it's a sound and the day is so quiet it feels like it's compressing me into stone.

In the distance, I see a flotilla of whale-watching boats. You can tell that's what they are, because they're bright yellow and orange and emblazoned with company names. I stand up to see better. If there are whale-watching boats, well, duh, there are obviously whales.

I make my way down to the point. It's covered with bladder wrack and green seaweed and millions and millions of blue mussel shells and barnacles, which give my feet something to grip on to, so that I don't slip. I go out as far as I can, and then I see them.

The whales are amazing.

There are dozens of them, fins rising out of the sea, leaping and breaching and spyhopping and flying above and through the water. The whale-watching boats push closer, like they do, but the whales ignore them, moving on together.

And the sound.

The sound of them huffing through their blowholes. The sound of their tails smashing down on the water. It's like they are putting on a show for us, but a real show, not one that's been choreographed by an employee of some crappy marine park somewhere. This is a show of strength, of what they can do, and I'm not going to lie, it takes my breath away.

I watch until they vanish in the distance, the boats stuck to them like magnets. I watch until even the boats disappear into the late-afternoon haze that rises off Vancouver, an exhalation of exhaust and filth into the sky.

Heading back, I see Kelby on the beach. Sitting where I was sitting, her feet in the same tide pool.

I raise my hand in greeting. She waves.

I make my way over to where she is.

"Hey," she says. "Some whales, huh."

"Yep," I say. "Some whales."

And then—don't ask me how or why—suddenly we're making out, she lying down on the rock and me above her, her lips pulling me down and in and over and under and oh my god, I mean, seriously, oh my god, it's like I'm falling through space, through the ocean floor, through the galaxy, through everything everything everything and it's amazing.

I don't know what

I think that I'm

I think it was because the whales were so beautiful or because summer was ending and the sky was a perfect blue and the rock was exactly the right amount of warm and we were alone on this island and out there, in the strait, was a shark and some whales, but seriously

Well, it was

I mean, I don't even really have words for how it was. How it is.

How we walk back to the cabin holding hands, her hand perfectly fitting into mine, the sun making her hair look like platinum silk, the air cooling on our skin like water slipping off the perfectly taut black-and-white skin of an orca in a full dive, vanishing under the bottle-green glassy surface of the Salish Sea.

IN THE MORNING, KELBY IS GONE.

"Back to Vancouver," Dad says.

"What?" I say. I am balancing a bowl of Cheerios in one hand, fending off Apollo with the other. He is jumping on my leg again and again. He wants to go for his morning run, which I usually take the dogs on before it gets too hot. His claws scratch my skin and I push him off, maybe a bit too hard.

"Watch it," Dad says. "Don't push them around. These dogs have been through enough."

"*Dad,*" I say. "Please don't tell me their sad rescue story again. I want to know where Kelby is—what happened?"

"You were asleep," he says. "I don't know how you slept through that."

I shrug. "I'm a heavy sleeper," I say. It's true. Our apartment is really noisy. I've learned to sleep through anything.

"Yeah," he says. "I guess, well, I mean the truth is that Darcy and I had a . . . fight."

"What?" I say. "A fight?"

"They left," he said. "They'll be back. But Darcy is pretty terrified about the shark, JC. Everyone is scared. It's a big deal. I've called fisheries and they said we shouldn't swim. And she's . . . I think at first she was mostly on your side. But now that she knows what the risks are, well, she's angry with you. I guess. I don't know. I stuck up for you, even though . . . well, you're my son! And now, I think we broke up." His voice catches in his throat and he lets out a sob. "We broke up. We did."

The bowl of Cheerios falls out of my hand and we both watch it splash to the floor.

"Dad," I mumble. "I'm sorry. I tried to tell everyone. When I first saw it, I really didn't think it was real. Then I *did* think it was. Then I thought it wasn't. No one wanted to hear me. Or believe me. Then I wasn't sure either. I was confused."

He holds up his hand. "Come on," he says. "I'm your dad. I get it. I don't think Darcy gets it, but you don't have to explain it to me."

"So they left?" I say. "Without saying goodbye?"

"I think she'll come back," he says. "I think they'll come back. It's . . . she's not like your mom. She doesn't mean it when she says she hates me."

"Neither did Mom!" I say.

"Oh, man," he says. "JC. She did mean it. With her everything was so fatal. So final. You know? You know how she is. But with Darcy." He sighs, runs his fingers through his hair. "I got her a ring," he tells me. "But who marries the underemployed-writer guy? What kind of influence would I be as a dad to those kids? Who would want that?"

"Hey," I say. "Dad. Come on. You're a good dad. You'd be great. Charlie loves you, and Kelby—" I think about it. "Well, she writes, too. You should read her book. Maybe you could help her. Or, I don't know, she could help you."

"Yeah," he says, slowly. "She does? She writes? Really? I didn't know that. She never said." He stares out the window. A tugboat is pulling a barge laden with wood chips slowly through the pass. It honks three times. "I really love her," he says. "I just really love her."

"I know, Dad," I say. Because I get it. I know he does. I know he loved Mom, too. But it was different. Because that's how it is. You can fall in love so hard with someone but it can be different from what you have with someone else. This is something I know: what I have with Daff is a supernova. Maybe it's destined to be a black hole. Maybe not. But what I have with Kelby? It's more like a meteor. Maybe it's the meteor I need to wipe the slate clean. But it's definitely a shooting-star kind of love. I swallow hard. I'm not going to cry.

But me and my dad, we're criers, I guess.

"I hope they come back," he says. "What if they don't come back?"

"Me too," I say. "They will, Dad."

"I didn't see the boat go out," he says. "Maybe she changed her mind."

"She probably did," I agree. "She wouldn't leave."

"Yeah," he says. "I'll walk up there in a while. I'll check."

Then Darcy is suddenly there, looking frantic, and Dad is saying, "I thought you'd left?"

And she's yelling, "I can't find Charlie! Charlie's gone!"

"What?" I say. "Where is he?" I get up too fast, the room tilting a bit before righting itself. Dad's hand is on my arm.

"Are you okay?" he says.

"I'm fine, where is he?" I say again.

"If I knew *that*, he wouldn't be missing," Darcy snaps. Then, "Sorry, I'm not mad at—anyway, we have to find him. Help me find him. Please, help me find him."

Dad is already slipping on his shoes, already half out the door with the dogs, screaming, "CHARLIE CHARLIE CHARLIE!" I hear them thundering down the path toward the beach.

It takes me a few minutes to get my head straight enough to follow them. I try to think like Charlie. The first thing I think of is the hotel. I climb up the trail, not calling him, but listening instead. The sounds are so pronounced here, you'd notice any rustle in the bushes, anything that isn't right. But I don't hear anything, just the thump of my bare feet on the packed trail.

The skeleton of the building rises toward the sky but doesn't get above the tree line. It looks like a drawing, superimposed on the trees. I'm calling Charlie but I'm thinking about meteors. About how one could hit me right now, right here.

And it would be the end of everything. The end of anything. The end of the everyanything.

"*Charlie*," I shout, but his absence is palpable. Not here, not here, not here.

But where?

I think about the shark.

No, not that.

I walk slowly back to the cabin, listening.

I'm almost at the small beach in front of our place when I hear him.

He's crying.

I look up. He's perched out on the end of a branch of the tree, way too far. Like I was, the first time he saw me practicing, showing off.

"Hey, kid," I say, trying to keep my voice calm. "What's up?"

"Oh hi," he says back. "I'm going to do what you did, okay?"

I try to keep my voice controlled. "No," I say. "It's a bit too far, buddy. It's too far to fall. You'll—" the word catches in my throat. "Hey, maybe back down to here a bit." I point farther back down the tree. I can't really see him because of where the sun is shining, that's the problem. He's a silhouette above me. Too far. Twenty feet maybe. He'd die if he jumped from there.

I'm suddenly desperate.

"Don't jump," I say. "Just wiggle backward, okay?"

"No," he says.

There was this one time, in a parking garage. Me and The King had been drinking a bit. We never drank to get drunk. We drank to get brave. Braver. "The bravest," he'd say, and raise his bottle, clinking it against mine. There was a gap between one parking garage and the next. And we were going to jump it. We were daring ourselves. We'd jumped way farther, both of us. We'd made it way farther than that. I don't know why it was so scary, but it was. Maybe twelve floors. Thirteen. I hadn't counted.

We skated for a while. To work up the nerve. A few beers. Some kind of fancy Canadian beer that his dad imported. He always had to have the best of whatever was available. This stuff tasted thick and bitter. Too strong. It was pretty disgusting.

The King went first and man, he really flew. His feet pulled up to his chest, he looked like someone in an action movie.

"That was tight," I yelled.

When it was my turn, I don't know what happened. Maybe the beer was too strong. Or maybe I wasn't that into it. I had to go home and write a report for English on a famous novel written in the twentieth century, which really left the door so far open that I hadn't been able to pick. I was supposed to meet Daff on the corner to go with her to this dinner at her parents' house because she needed a date and The King had turned her down. I was thinking about too much stuff is really all it was. Anyway, when I took off, I knew I'd gone wrong. My legs were too heavy and in the gap between the buildings, they felt like an anchor I'd thrown overboard. I would probably have died but I somehow grabbed a pipe, a stupid rusty pipe, and held on. I dangled there until he ran out of that building and back into the one I was in. It took ages, my hands slipping, sweaty on the pipe. I thought I was going to fall for sure.

And I was tired of being about to fall.

When The King died, I'd been thinking of telling him it was enough.

I'd been thinking of asking him about that day, about why he didn't just jump back the way he'd gone, to get to me sooner.

It was like he almost hesitated. It was like he almost wondered what that would look like, if I fell.

I swallow hard. I won't cry. Now is not the time.

"You've got to come down," I call to Charlie. "Slow, okay? No tricks."

"It's not a trick, it's a skill, dog," he says, quoting me back to me.

He looks like an angel silhouetted against the sun like that. And I do the only thing I can do, which is hold out my arms and catch him when he falls.

Which he does. Hard.

Both of us falling onto the rocks, but he's in my arms and he's alive and he's okay and he's crying and I'm crying, and the whole world is crying, wet drops of rain falling from the gray, almost-autumn sky, those goddamn trees starting to abscise their leaves all around us, the leaves falling like so much bright confetti against the dull veil of clouds.

46

I ONLY HAVE A FEW MORE DAYS ON THE ISLAND WHEN
the tide brings in the body.

The adolescent great white shark—because that's what it is—
comes in on the highest tide of the year. It happens in the middle
of the night, so that when we go down to the beach in the morning
for our swim, he's hidden at first by the rock where we sit and read
and lie in the sun and sometimes make out but not anymore.

But the smell is unbelievable and unmistakable. What death
smells like is instantly recognizable, even if you haven't ever smelled
death before. Every cell in your body knows that odor and reacts to
it with a recoiling that begins somewhere so deep inside you couldn't
even guess which organ started the rush, but you want to run far
and fast and get away from that.

Fight that instinct.

Stay.

It's Kelby who finds him first, climbing up onto the rock, looking down on the other side, gasping.

"Oh my god," she says. "Oh my god, oh my god, oh my god." And then she's on her knees and I have to force my eyes to look where she's pointing, to see what she's seeing.

It's just that the shark is so big and so destroyed and so utterly completely dead that he couldn't be more dead if he'd fallen off a steel beam on the forty-second floor of a building that his dad was constructing on the corner of Eleventh and Fifty-Third. The body of the shark is splayed and awkwardly bent, broken in too many places. Most of his meat is missing, leaving behind a frame with some skin hanging, his flat eyes shielded by the second lid, like he knew what was coming and braced himself for it as best he could.

His fin is still attached.

I go down to the sand even though the smell is unbearable. To be so close. I reach over the falling-apart carcass and put my hand on his fin. It feels cool and firm and solid, like the trunk of an arbutus tree, like a human leg, like anything.

Like everything.

I hold tight to the fin, tears streaming down my face.

The thing is, I don't have anyone to blame. I want to blame someone.

"Oh my god," I say, too, because what else is there to say really. Above us, circling, there are turkey vultures. At first only three, then four, then five. They are waiting for us to step away. They are ready to feast on this, what's left of it.

"NO," I yell at them. "NO."

"Calm down," says Kelby. "Screaming isn't going to help."

"Nothing is going to help," I say. "Are you crazy? He's dead. It's dead. She. Whatever."

"I'm not crazy," she says, shaking her head. "I'm pretty normal." She grins.

"Right," I say. "Me too."

She stares at me and man, I want to kiss her. What is wrong with me that I want to kiss her now?

"This guy stinks," she says. "But he's something. Isn't he something?"

"Yeah," I say. "No kidding."

I'm still holding his fin. I don't know how to let go. The smell feels like it has moved through me and I don't know how to move my legs or arms and the fin is cool and slightly dry and yet also slippery in my hand and then Kelby is standing in front of me and then her arms are around me and then I'm kissing her again because she's there and nothing makes sense.

Eventually, I let go of the fin and then we're lying down in the sand and rotting flesh from the shark is beside us and on us and under us and I don't care.

I thought our story would end differently from this, that's the thing. When you meet a person and then you like a person and you start to notice stuff about a person, like their eyelashes or the way their ears kind of wiggle when they laugh or how they are always cupping their knees when they are sitting down and talking or how they always look up at just the right second to catch the shooting star, when that happens, you think your story is going to be super-romantic and end in some kind of super-romantic way. Not with you actually becoming related. Not with your parents getting married. Not like that.

But even while I'm lying there with Kelby, on Kelby, in Kelby, on the sand, by the shark, the dead shark, I know this is our ending and I hate it. I hate it so much. I hate it in a way that I've never hated anything before and I lean down and I kiss her forehead and I say, "I know it probably doesn't count but I love you." And she says, "I love you, too," and that's sort of better and sort of not because I get up and walk away, whistling for the dogs who are up behind the logs, staying far away from that death, decomposing and forgiveness back there below the tide line where the pebbles turn into sinking sand that soon will be covered up again with the cold green water from the strait.

I don't look back. I don't know how long she stayed. I don't know what she was waiting for, what else she needed from me, what else I could have said.

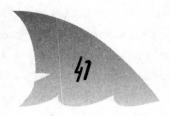

47

THE SHARK WAS KILLED BY ORCAS. THAT'S WHAT THE
fisheries guy says when he finally shows up. His body was torn
apart by the whales. The shark was really young, probably only a
few months old, and somehow off his migratory path. Maybe he
was mixed up because of the climate change and the warm current, maybe he was exploring, figuring out a different route. Maybe
his mom died and left him directionless. Maybe someone killed
her for sport or maybe the ocean killed her, with everything in it
that's broken.

Or maybe someone murdered her for her fins, leaving her body
to sink slowly to the ocean floor. Leaving this baby to wonder what
happened. To find his own way.

He found his way to *dead*.

I stood beside him in knee-deep water while the fisheries man
explained everything and nothing. Darcy came down for a bit and
listened and then she prayed on the rock, her back to us, kneeling
to the sun. If I'd had my phone, that would have been the best

Instagram shot of the year. The way the sun shone down, like it was shining a spotlight on her. I don't know about praying, but I know what's beautiful. So does Dad, I guess. He proposed.

She said, "Yes." I don't know when it happened and Dad isn't talking, he's tight-lipped but smiling, and I get it, I do. But I'm still sad because, Mom. And because, everything.

The shark wasn't really that big, maybe nine feet from nose to tail. He looked so huge in the water. He looked like everything I've ever believed in and couldn't save.

I took a tooth. It wasn't easy. I had to wait until the fisheries guy was busy in his boat, organizing other fisheries guys to prepare nets to haul the shark away. I pried the tooth out of his mouth with Kelby's pocketknife. It was like trying to pull a table leg off a table, it was stuck so firm. I cut my finger really deeply. It started to bleed in a way that would have been scary a few months ago but now didn't mean anything. My finger. My blood. The tinny taste of it in my mouth.

"*Sorry,*" I whispered, and that sorry stretched out so far between me and the shark that the invisible thread stretched to infinity and to heaven and to wherever the spirit of stuff goes when it dies because it has to go somewhere, and I think it got all the way to The King, that's how far it went. I cried, now waist deep in the rising tide, and the corpse of the shark was tethered to the fisheries boat, to be dragged somewhere for scientists to study and destroy and take pictures of for the local news.

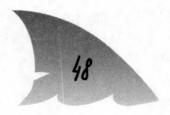

48

BACK AT THE CABIN, I OPENED THE E-MAILS FROM DAFF, one by one.

It took me a while to read through them all, but then I got to the one with the attachment.

I got to the one with the letter from The King.

I got to the thing I never wanted to see but now I couldn't help it. There was nothing I could do to protect myself from it anymore. There was nothing I wanted to do.

I opened it.

I read it.

Finally, I went up to the loft and packed my stuff. I loaded it into the boat and I waited for Dad to be ready to take me in. I'm not good at goodbyes, that's the thing. I'm just not. He was pretty quiet. I mean, there wasn't much to say.

At the airport, when he hugged me, I didn't even flinch. I hugged him back.

"I really liked the book, Dad," I said. "Maybe you should put a shark in it."

"Yeah," he said. "Think I will, kid."

And that was it. I guess you were probably expecting more, but it was just another chapter that ended differently from how I would have thought.

It just stopped.

Dad waved and got into his stupid purple car, which choked and spluttered but finally started, calling like a mateless whale into the evening light.

I walked into the airport and got ready to go home, the shark's tooth in my pocket, pressing sharply against the summer-tanned flesh of my thigh.

49

Dude,

   I don't know how to write a suicide note. I Googled it.
Which made me even more sure that I wanted to kill
myself. Because seriously, you can Google suicide notes.
You can Google how to write a suicide note. What is the
point in any one life when any answer you can possibly seek
can be found on Google? I found this poem, which is
apparently a famous suicide poem. Maybe you should start
by reading this poem that I didn't write. I didn't write any
poems. So already this guy's life, I guess, was worth more
than mine:

   Delicate line between heaven and earth . . .
   The calm of the ages,
   all the world's worth.
   Such minuscule measure,
   while we think it so grand . . .

Just five specks of smallness,
This soft quiet land.
So frail and so fleeting,
in the end you will see
Simple dreams were Horatio's philosophy.

For all the truth,
all creation,
all secrets of yore
Can be told in an instant,
by then they're no more.

Ah, The Unexplainable
All worries unsettled,
heartache unresolved . . .
All questions unanswered,
with death, shall be solved.

We already teeter,
this sheer cliff so high.
When we fall to corruption,
insecurities die.

To end is to start;
to surrender is to know.

Despair and depression,
together they grow.

Hope shall meet hopeless
when there's nowhere to go.

Is that beautiful? I thought it was when I found it on
Wikipedia, but now I don't know. Maybe I don't know
what beauty is anymore. What is it? Some freaking flower?
The way someone looks? Light? I don't remember. I can't
find it. There's no beauty here for me, you know? When I
hold it up and inspect it, that dumb poem looks kind of
thin on the ground, if you know what I mean. Crappy,
overworked. But that last bit: hope shall meet hopeless
when there's nowhere to go. That's the truth.

The only poem I ever liked is that one we rapped for
Mr. D. Remember that one? I can't remember the whole
thing, but I remember the last part, my part:

we're anything brighter than even the sun
(we're everything greater
than books
might mean)
we're everyanything more than believe
(with a spin
leap
alive we're alive)
we're wonderful one times one

Sharky, we were so fucking bright, like the sun. I don't
want you to think . . .

I don't know. You, me, and Daff. We were everything. But you know what? It would have ended. We would have grown up. Everything was about to change. You and Daff were gonna be You and Daff. And I was gonna just be me.

But that's not the reason. It's one of the reasons.

When people ask you why, you can say: because reasons.

I was scared all the time. I was so freaking scared. Reasons.

Here's some other stuff that I Googled:

1. How to tell your best friend that you're gay.

2. How to not be your father.

Then I realized, for real, that I'd rather die than do it. Not telling you. I could have told you. I should have. I don't know why I had to. I could have told you that I was in love with you. It would have been easy. So easy. I thought telling my dad was the hardest thing, but it wasn't. He already hated me because I was exactly like him. You get that, right? I was exactly like him. I was not going to be that man. No way. No how. But I was. It was already too late. All that genetic material of him knitting together to make me, him, me, him, make me into him.

That's who I'm never going to be, buddy. I'm not. I couldn't stop it though. I was already such a jerk. I already hated myself. I wasn't good enough for you, even if you were gay, too, which I know you weren't. And I got that. I was okay with that. You're an amazing guy though. God, I could have loved you. But you would have hated me eventually, because I would have become him. He was bigger than all of us. He was the biggest thing. The every everything. You know?

This letter needs editing but fuck that. I don't have to make it good. It's a suicide note, not a paper that's gonna get me into college, like I couldn't have had my pick of schools anyway, because Dad.

Death just sounds a lot more interesting to me than reenacting his effing script. You and I both know how it would have gone. I would have slowly become less likable but would have gotten more friends. I would have had more money and less taste. I would have stopped caring about the stuff that matters, stuff that you and Daff care about, like the goddamn rain forest. I already don't care about it. I know on some level that I should, but I don't. I'm already him.

I am him.

My dad is the only person in the world who I ever hated, except for me.

I was always jealous that you had a mom. I think if I had a mom, I wouldn't be like this.

I'm really freaking broken, Sharkboy. I don't think you had any idea. Have any idea. Will ever have any idea.

You know when I first met you and I said you were going to be a hero, because you're the underdog? I was lying. Not about the heroism, but about the underdog. You're no underdog, man. You were born to be the hero, all six feet tall and noble and good and all that other crap that at first I thought couldn't be for real, but is. It is real. You are already a hero, you idiot. There is nothing heroic about being rich, it's just something that happens when you don't give one single damn about anyone but yourself. But there's something heroic about you and your stupid sharks and the way you just go ahead and cry in front of everyone in the world because one day you might suffocate when the plankton runs out. You are insane, kid. I would have traded places with you in an instant.

Hear me out:

This is your future: you are going to change things. You're going to be the goddamn Time magazine Man of the Year one day. You're Harry freakin' Potter, but you have no idea that you are. You think you're just a Muggle. (And yeah, I know you didn't get my thing with that book, but what can I say? It was a good book. A good series of books. You might not get this, but a guy like me is going to wish he was a kid who could go to wizarding school, who is living in the wrong family by mistake, but there's something better out there. That's what I wanted: Hogwarts. Which isn't real. Everything I wanted wasn't real. Do you get it?)

You're a wizard.

This is my future: I am going to crash and burn. I am going to be tabloid fodder. I am going to act out the same story of rich-kid-gone-wrong that every rich-kid-gone-wrong has acted out before me and I'm so goddamn bored of that story already and I can't do it. I can't do it. Sharky, listen,

I'm already blowing congressmen in the bushes. I am already so far down I can't see the surface from down here and I've told you a million times, black guys don't swim.

I can't swim.

I don't even want to swim.

I'm not going to do it. I don't want to do it. I'm sorry but I'm not cut out to do it. Everything is a choice.

I'm choosing.

Now I'm going to steal from someone else's letter. It's not plagiarism. Or it is, but who is going to give one single damn? Is someone going to sue me in the grave? Well, probably. But screw it.

Hopefully, they'll sue my old man.

Hopefully, he'll lose.

Here it is:

If anybody could have saved me it would have been you. Everything has gone from me but the certainty of your goodness. I can't go on spoiling your life any longer. I don't think two people could have been happier than we have been.

That's the truth, JC. That's what I would have written if Virginia Woolf didn't think of it first. You are good.

This last jump, this final parkour party trick, this is going to be everything. This is going to be the real me. Finally. Out there. At last.

You won't believe me. I know you won't believe me. Not when you see what you'll see and goddamnit, I don't want you to but I'm also as selfish as anything and I do want you to because I don't want to go alone and I love you. I love you. I love you and I always will.

And not in a gay way.

Okay, sort of in a gay way.

What you need to know is that what I'm going to be feeling is free. I'm going to be so freaking happy on that ride. It's going to be the fall of a lifetime.

The ride is the thing.

I'm sorry, Great White Hero. You don't believe me, but it's true.

I'm sick. Sick of all the bullshit. Sick of pretending. Sick of the world. Sick of being broken. I'm taking all the broken things and making them into a parachute, just like Mr. B. taught us.

Except parachutes are for sissies.

I've got to go.

Love,

Marvin ("The King") Johnston III

50

THE FRENCH WORD FOR "THE END" IS FIN.

This feels just about as important as anything else as you make
your way down the crowded sidewalk toward the iron gates of the
Academy of Rich Gods and Goddesses of the World on the first
day of your senior year. Your shoes look too new and shiny and they
hurt your heels. Your feet would like to reject the shoes. You'd
like to drop your backpack and make your way up and over that
fence, there, beyond that brownstone to that alley to that garden
to maybe a park where you could find a tree and climb it, your back
arching against the pain where the branch rests. You'd flip over and
back, free-falling for just a second before being jarred back to earth
by the way your feet hurt when you land. You'd take off your tie and
start to run. Maybe you'd get to the subway, maybe not, maybe the
subway would go to a beach. Maybe when you got there, you'd take
off your stupid shoes and socks and even your pants and tie and shirt
and jacket and then maybe you'd walk into the sea. Maybe you'd

swim. Maybe you'd hold your breath and go deep and maybe, just maybe, you'd see something under the water: a girl or a shark or both. And maybe that would change everything forever or for now.

Or maybe you'll keep walking. Maybe when you get to the school, your best friend, Daffodil Blue, of recent *Gawker* fame and "It Girl" status, will be sitting on the front steps, her hair tufted up around her head in her signature 'fro that half the class is sporting. Or maybe she'll have shaved her head, to make a statement. The kind of statement that says, *Yeah? Well, copy* this *if you dare*. Maybe she'll be waiting for you. Maybe you'll say, *Hey*. Maybe she'll say, *Hey yerself, Sharkman*. And maybe you'll walk into the school together, touching but not touching, close enough that you can smell how she smells this year, like lemon soap and cloves and slightly of salty sea air. Maybe she'll say, *Lunch at Mo's*. Maybe you'll agree. Maybe the two of you will invent a complicated gang handshake, right there in the entrance of the school, just because.

Maybe there will be a plaque in the front lobby and a photo of The King. Maybe it will be some kind of memorial. Maybe you'll look at it and your stomach will fall, like you're dropping from a great height and maybe you'll feel something like nausea or panic or maybe you'll try to understand what he meant by joy. Maybe you'll excuse yourself after the bell goes and go into the bathroom where you'll be alone. Maybe after you wash your hands, you'll look up and see yourself in the mirror and there, standing behind you, will be a funny-looking black kid with a cigarette in his hands. Maybe the kid will say, "So, heeeee-ro, what'll it be this year?" Maybe you'll blink and he'll be gone.

Then maybe, just maybe, you'll take your new phone out of

your pocket. You'll be breathing too shallow and too fast. You'll need oxygen. You'll take a photo and send it to someone who maybe lives in Canada, someone who is about to be your *stepsister*, a girl with a halo of platinum hair. Maybe you'll type, *I saw a ghost. I saw a star. #ghostsarejuststarswestillsee #Igetit #Imissyou*

Maybe then you'll straighten your tie a bit and dry your hands. When you look in the mirror, maybe you'll see that you look like your dad. Maybe you won't hate this. Maybe you'll think, My dad is one of the good guys. And you'll smile a little bit at yourself because he is and you are.

Maybe then you'll be able to breathe slowly enough that you can walk into class. You can say, *Good to see you, man.* You can say, *Dude, good summer?* And maybe when someone asks you the same question then you'll be able to smile and say, *Yes.*

ACKNOWLEDGMENTS

I don't know how old I was when I read Peter Benchley's *Jaws*. I want to say I was pretty young. Too young, definitely. And it was the book, not the movie, that really did me in. (For the record, I'm still too young for the movie.) From that day forward, whenever I was in the ocean (which was a lot! I lived on an island), I just waited for the shadow that always lurked below me to show itself to be the great white shark that was waiting to bite me. Even when it didn't make sense. Especially when it didn't make sense. As I grew up, I read everything I could about this fish that instilled so much terror in me as a child. I stopped being afraid. Most importantly, I learned that sharks rarely bite people. This year (I'm writing this in 2015), there have been an unusual number of shark bites reported, and this is due to a conflagration of issues: climate change, overfishing, more people in the ocean, swimmers at beaches that are also baited for fishing, and murky water. The list goes on. The facts remain unchanged though: sharks are not out to get us. Having survived five major extinctions, sharks are simply going about the business of surviving, just like the rest of us. The shark-finning industry has almost entirely emptied the ocean of the majority of its sharks. No one can say with 100 percent certainty what happens when an apex predator is removed from the food chain, but we know that it will have far-reaching implications.

The people behind the documentary *Sharkwater* (sharkwater.com) are making a difference. Shark activists around the world are making a difference. But it might be too little, too late. Please consider throwing your own loud voice in with the rising chorus who are working to shut down the shark-finning industry. This book is for them and for you and for all of us who hope to continue to survive on a planet that we are very quickly depleting of sharks (and everything else, for that matter).

If nothing else, I hope you start paying attention. Say no to shark fin soup and restaurants that serve it. Please.

In addition to the people who are working tirelessly for change, I owe a debt of gratitude to all the people who made this particular novel possible: Jennifer Laughran (for everything), Janine O'Malley and the rest of the team at FSG (for loving and supporting the book), the Canada Council for the Arts, my readers (of course!), my kids (who remind me every day why I do this and why it's important to use my voice to speak out when I can), and last, but not least, my wonderful parents (for providing me with the setting of this book and of so many others). It's the best place in the world. I'd set everything there, if only I could.

Quite often, people ask me why I write young adult books. I tell them that it's because my teen years were the most vivid of my life. When you're a teenager, everything feels truly real for the first time. You are figuring out who you are going to be and how that's going to happen, how you'll go from kid-you to your true self. It can be a difficult journey, no lie. High school is hard. Sometimes you have disastrous relationships, make horrible mistakes, or suffer such painful humiliations that it's hard to see past them. Sometimes the road to who you want to be looks impassable, filled with too many obstacles, too many naysayers, too many haters. Sometimes it looks like the best option is to opt out. I am one of many voices who are here to tell you—to *promise* you—that it gets better. It absolutely, 100 percent gets better. Even when it seems impossible. Even when you don't believe that it can. It can. And it will. But if you're struggling with how and why, I just ask that you reach out to someone, anyone who can help you, or at least, try to help you. If you don't have anyone in your life who fits the bill, please call a help line, such as the National Suicide Prevention Lifeline at 1-800-273-TALK (1-800-273-8255), or visit a website like itgetsbetter.org.

Sometimes life is really, really hard. But I promise that it's not impossible forever. There's joy. Not every day, and maybe not yet, but eventually it finds you. I swear. Stay strong. I believe in you.